DIARY
OF A BLOOD
DONOR

Originally published in Estonian as *Doonori meelespea* by Kupar, 1990

Library of Congress Cataloging-in-Publication Data

Unt, Mati.
[Doonori meelespea. English]
Diary of a blood donor / Mati Unt ; translation by Ants Eert.
    p. cm.
"Originally published in Estonian as Doonori meelespea by Kupar, 1990."
ISBN-13: 978-1-56478-496-4 (alk. paper)
ISBN-10: 1-56478-496-7 (alk. paper)
I. Eert, Ants. II. Title.
PH666.31.N75D6613 2008
894'.54532--dc22
                                    2007044884

Special thanks to the Estonian Literature Information Centre and Traducta for supporting the translation of this novel.

Partially funded by a grant from the National Endowment for the Arts, a federal agency, the Illinois Arts Council, a state agency, and by the University of Illinois, Urbana-Champaign

www.dalkeyarchive.com

DIARY
OF A BLOOD
DONOR

by Mati Unt
Translated from the Estonian by Ants Eert

Dalkey Archive Press
Champaign and London

I

Decisive, she approaches
The high tower, intending
To cast herself off the top [. . .]
But unexpectedly the tower spoke.
—Apuleius, "The Marriage of Cupid and
Psyche," *The Golden Ass*

AN UNEXPECTED INVITATION

A crow was riding the wind that came in low over the beach. Sand blew through the window, landed on my papers, entered my mouth. A yellowish light tainted the room, even my fingers. I carefully reread the letter from this morning's mail, but it remained impenetrable. A complete stranger, writing in Russian, wanted me to meet him next Sunday in Leningrad where the cruiser *Aurora* was docked.

Next Sunday, Leningrad, *Aurora*?

A week from now, hundreds of kilometers from Tallinn?

What's going on?

Having explained nothing, the letter's last line threatened: This meeting is vital.

It was unsigned.

The kind of letter that should go right into the garbage. Except . . .

Except:

Vital for whom? For me? Him?

Is it an emergency?

Have I inherited a fortune?

Am I dealing with a spy?

A seductive woman?

A wealthy foreign publisher?

What have I overlooked?

Are they luring me away to be murdered?

Is it an admirer of my novels?

Or some poor bastard about to die?

Army counterespionage?

I put the letter away again, and for the third time decided not to go anywhere. Am I a marionette to be yanked around on a string? An anonymous letter arrives and immediately I get ready to run off on a fool's errand.

Who's the fool?

Apparently it's me.

As an obscure writer, freedom fighters and spies tend to ignore me. It's true that once in a while letters come to enlighten me on some brand-new world order or synergy, with copious details appended. But the cruiser *Aurora*, the cradle of revolution, the ship that fired the shot on October 25, 1917, signaling the beginning of the assault on the Winter Palace—what's it got to do with me? Sure, my life has been affected by that infamous shot, but so have the lives of the thousands of people around me. Will all of us now be called to the *Aurora*? Perhaps it's only those who approve of the revolution? Or only those who disapprove? If I alone was invited, how was I selected?

No, this is just a silly joke. Or maybe revenge? But for what?

What have I done?

Everyone's guilty of something—am I any guiltier than anyone else?

That's it: I'm going to ignore the letter.

Using the last packet my Finnish publisher had sent me, I brewed some coffee, added sugar I had obtained with my ration card, and to steady my shaky nerves, invented all sorts of excuses for doing nothing: gas stations are out of gas, trains are overbooked, buses are overcrowded—I can't travel at all, our Great State is in a lot of trouble. Gas has all but disappeared because the rail services that bring it in have been almost completely shut down. Public transportation is bone dry too. Am I supposed to walk to Leningrad? I do have some bread left; no point in going to the grocery, since there's also a sausage shortage on. Shortages promote self-reliance. At least something good has come out of this mess, thank God: There's nothing to be gained by going out. Let them write and invite. I'll withdraw, learn to know myself, tell the world to go to hell; I can't be bothered watching the end of the world, won't cry at its grave. Far better to stay on the sofa with its springs poking me in the ass—there are no upholsterers available, and anyway no sofa covers. I do have some soap saved up, a whole cake; I've even hoarded a tube of toothpaste. There's no way

I'm going down to the cruiser *Aurora*. I'll ignore everyone and everything. Of course, poverty and lack of means shouldn't really be an excuse for turning one's back on adventure. A colleague of mine recently visited North Korea, and another one went to Mongolia. Far away corners of the world, where the sun is hot and the people and their habits are inscrutable. Going to the cruiser would be a new experience, no? I might get a short story out of it, or the beginning of a novel? The last living member the Czar's family wants to reveal everything to me, yet here I sit, stretched out on a shabby sofa, protecting my ivory tower.

What if terrorists are planning to blow up the cruiser, and I'd have a front-row seat for the event? Front-row seat? Or maybe I'd be blown up with the ship?

I'm not sticking my neck out.

Still, I guess the ship could sail and take me along. I've written about the ships and the sea. I did write a commemorative article on Lennart Meri, but that hardly qualifies me as a naval historian.

Am I being accosted by a radical organization getting ready to set off another revolution and planning to blow up the *Aurora* in order to publicize their cause? And afterwards they'll supervise a ceremonial casting of flowers onto the waves? And make endless, boring speeches? But in that case the letter would have had a declaration in it, a slogan or two. If I was being courted by revolutionaries, I would've been invited to a bar in some dank cellar, not a pier. So, could it be a woman who adores me? But in that case the letter would have had at least a few loving words in it—especially since I'm known to be such a sucker for sentimentality. A homosexual, perhaps? I've never been mistaken for one, and in any case, the symbolism here—a long ship with big guns and a proud prow splitting the waves—is just too obvious.

Could it be something to do with the subconscious? The Flying Dutchman? Long John Silver? Moby Dick? The ship of transcendence, its mast pointing up at the North Star, following the axis of the Earth? Could it be I've been invited to the White Ship that everyone is waiting for, the ship that never comes to our shores except to bring us across the Styx?

But the letter is matter of fact. Fine sand settles on my papers. I stand at the window.

INSPIRATION

Wandering around the town, I happened to meet some friends of mine, and despite being eager to mention the letter, I felt as though I'd been told to keep my mouth shut. Although the letter-writer hadn't said his invitation was a secret, he could be testing my character. In any case, would my friends believe me? They might think I was drunk or playing a practical joke on them. Many of them have received invitations to strange places, like the symposium of Supreme Soviets: lands inhabited by pagans, the PEN Club, torture chambers, and auctions of Picasso's art. An invitation to the *Aurora* wouldn't rate very high on that list.

In the Estbrilliant display window, a fly was crawling among the shiny gems tastefully arranged on dark blue velvet—God's creature, but worthless. What a provocation, for a fly to display itself along with all those valuables! What audacity! So what was the matter with me? While I was doing nothing, some twenty thousand brave men were going to their deaths to conquer a strip of land too small to hold their graves. Did I lack motivation, will, and strength? Greatness means being willing to perform great deeds, whether or not one has a good reason for doing them. Leaving Estbrilliant, I went up to the cabstand, where, naturally, around fifty people were already waiting in line.

Inspiration fails me, in my novels, when the time comes to describe a cabstand. I should write about the long, expectant line, my own wait, and then, during the first ten kilometers of my taxi ride, the scenery outside the window, the suburbs of an old Hansa town by the Gulf of Finland, now inhabited by half a million people.

It's horrifying that I'm still not able to do such things.

My hand won't respond.

To describe this scene is still beyond my powers.

But I won't insult Tallinn with some half-baked fantasy, either.

That's why my trip home has to remain vague and undescribed.

On the radio Tiina Kirs prognosticated on the approaching demise of postmodernism. Although her presentation was quite intelligent, she failed to rise above the level of other pedants whose last hope was a future where everything was different, where there were more freedoms and fewer restrictions. Still, most people prefer a routine life—it's not just a human trait but an animalistic one as well. A jaguar hates to be caged up in a zoo, although my learned opponent will point out that many jaguars become used to their cages. I'm not sure if I even want to be free. Freedom is so burdened with agitators and obstructionists, sometimes you just want to find refuge in autism, bury your head in sand, stop breathing altogether. What do I remember about the world out there? A helicopter was flying over my front lawn; I looked up hoping it would crash. I didn't wish the pilot any harm. But, barely moving my lips, I whispered: fall, fall, fall. Of course, the helicopter didn't crash. People stroll by my house. How do they fit into the big picture? What picture? The picture of what we've all chosen, what we've agreed to. What's out, what's in? Love, for instance, I can say is definitely *in*, also flavor, good or bad— not only flavor of food but also the taste of blood in my mouth after brushing my teeth with a stiff brush. Anyway, this could be a starting point.

But a starting point for what?

What a silly question.

Without a doubt, it would have to be creativity.

A man wakes up in the evening mistaking a sunset for dawn.

A lost stranger knocks on a woman's door.

A wife cooks supper for her cheating husband. She's waiting for him at the window.

I might write about amnesia.

And Anderson.

About the men and women who populate the countryside.

Reality.

Simultaneous events.

About a hyperactive old man in a wasteland.

Why not?

It would be a way to escape that cruiser with its loaded guns, awaiting me.

Consider the fact that many scenes start nowhere and end nowhere. Never mind theoretically—I mean in real life. That's how it is in my own life. Other people may have had different experiences in life. That cloud in the sky, when did it appear? I never noticed, but there it is. Should I wait for the cloud to disappear? I get out of bed and a swarm of mosquitoes attacks me, coming in through the window to suck my blood, and later the sun will set. Does that cloud have a beginning and an end, I ask like a child who's joined a philosophy class halfway through the class. Let's take marriages, for example—my own or anyone's. Familiarity grows and grows, but eventually a crisis arises, a crisis with its roots in the past, still hanging around. Outside the window of the cab a face flashes past with a finger up its nose; that person also has a story but we can't get involved: by the time we'd brake, we'd be long past him. A bum begs for money, a glowworm under a bush emits its phosphorescence, and the people who mistake those worms for snakes avoid them. The woods are empty, the leaves rustle while we lie down, scratch ourselves, wake at dawn, wait a few seconds for our souls to catch up with our bodies, and life goes on like clockwork.

A PICTURE FROM MY YOUTH

The cruiser *Aurora* fired her gun on the night of October 25, 1917, and after that she toured Helsinki and Kronstadt. In 1946 she became an icon on the Neva River.

Many old ships have earned their retirements.

The "Oseberg" Viking ship near Oslo.

Fitzcarraldo's ship in the rain forest.

The following happened in a youth camp at Värska in 1964.

I've forgotten the names of the camp commandant and his staff, but I do remember that the project was progressive. None of us were there looking for glory or an easy way up the bureaucratic ladder by supporting the prevailing ideology. A few of us were in our twenties, but most were still in middle school, barely fifteen years old. I do remember Mark Soosaar—now a film director—who at that time was an MC on the radio. I remember Mati Polder and Aare Tiisvälja too—they were television personalities. But things were different in those days. At night we caught crawdads, which may or may not have been a prohibited activity. We had lively discussions by the campfire, but the gist of our arguments, unfortunately, has escaped me. But I repeat: we were certainly progressive.

Värska, in the extreme Southeast of Estonia, is in a province of Setumaa. No wonder then that the wasteland there, where practically nothing grows, is called the Setumaa Sahara.

One day we took a walk in that desert. To avoid the heat we set out at dawn, but when the sun came up, the cooling wind disappeared. Scraggy bushes offered no shade. We walked for a long time. Sweat poured off us, and the water cans were empty. Exactly where we went I have no idea. No one wanted to be the first one to quit. On the contrary, the stronger people in the group seemed to be enjoying the misery of the weaker. We did pass a couple of farmsteads, where no one was to be seen. Duke Ellington's "Caravan" sounded from one of their windows. It suited the occasion. We kept on going through the parched vegetation. Far away we heard some explosions— probably the Russian Air Force conducting exercises on the lake. Why a lake? Explosions over water sound different. Then, the figure of a fleshy, sun-baked, half-naked man appeared out of nowhere. He spoke gibberish, vaguely like our own language, but we didn't understand a single word. Had his tongue been cut out? Lonely places guard many secrets, and witnessing something illegal can be dangerous. Perhaps his attacker was humane. Instead of killing him, he just made sure the witness couldn't tell tales. How much can one reveal by waving one's arm? Had we accidentally stumbled on some high political conspiracy? Or perhaps the man was drunk? Was there another possibility? The bravest among us indicated that we were thirsty. The man made agreeable noises, beckoned. After some hesitation we followed him. Surprise! Behind a bush was a boat half buried in sand. Two of the side planks were broken, and on the board where the rower would normally sit, a lizard lazed in the sun—it quickly escaped. Our guide sat in the boat and took to rowing with imaginary oars. Was he acting out how he, in some gray time, arrived here, or would in some golden time depart? The man muttered something, as if inviting us to board the boat. We raised a cloud of dust getting away from him. Soon we were on our own again. It was possible that a long time ago this had been the shore of the lake. Maybe the boat had belonged to the grandfather of the tongueless man, a guerilla in the last war, who had needed to hide his boat from the enemy?

Somehow we made it back to the camp. In the cool of the evening, we rowed across the river to a nearby camp of university students. We lit a fire on the bank of the river with two friendly young women and tried to get kissed—but nothing; I think they were each keeping an eye on the other. When it began to rain, we rowed back to our own camp. By this time the eastern sky was blushing red. On the way I quoted Ristikivi: *After you left, you became a dream, but in my bed, my suffering continued.* The morning brought on more philosophical discussions; we all voted for increased middle-school and university-student autonomy. That day was just as hot.

> Having fashioned a grave
> From the sea, darkness exudes
> Terror where a whale-like
> *Aurora* haunts the night.
> —Vladimir Mayakovsky

WHY?

I came home in the evening, thunder in the air. Took off my shoes, locked the door, and drank some water. Thinking: would it be better if my people took to wilting at dawn like the flowers of the Queen of the Night? It would be terrible, but perpetual ignorance is also terrible. When will it end? When can we say: enough? No one knows. Just before the end of the millennium? Right after? On the phone, you just hear a sarcastic laugh. What kind of life it that? Is there no alternative? The West is not a useful model. Westerners no longer know what they want. But maybe they do? Apparently they do, but they won't enlighten us. During this masochistic conversation with myself, I felt that something was wrong. I checked my front room, waking up the yawning cat. He was satisfied with the situation. Then I noticed that the TV was on and the set was tuned to channel zero. I had definitely left the TV off. The cat? Absurd. I took him in my lap and looked deep into his eyes. He tolerated my gaze without flinching. His heart was pure. Unlike me, he was not a political animal. Who could have turned on my TV and put on channel zero? A thief? But nothing was stolen. My head began to ache. The cares of this world are heavy. A person has to be so many things at the same time: *Homo sapiens*, an Estonian, a nursing mother, a biped. I've listed only a tiny fraction of the full range of possibilities.

If I don't go, the letter will haunt me till I die. How did I overlook that one fundamental point? And if this meeting is so important, more letters will follow. And then revenge? They'll throw rocks through my windows. My boss will fire me. At night the chairs in my living room will start moving on their own. Editors will reject my work. A roof tile will fall and hit me on the head. The Great Unknown is rife with possibilities, and has many ways to get at you.

AFTER THE STORM, MINNI

After the lightning had lit up my ceiling and the thunder faded, I got out of bed around two o'clock in the morning to observe a strip of lavender sky poke out from under a cloud. I waited for something to happen, waited until my eyes began to water. As the cloud crept over the sea, more empty sky appeared. I cracked open the window. Cold air brushed my stomach. You watch the sky, I told myself, and you'll never know if it's for the last time. The sky doesn't care. The tenant across the street put on his lights, came out on the balcony. A feeling of ease had embraced the locals. Weird things had been going on during thunderstorms lately—clocks would stop, especially pendulum clocks, and an owl came to squat on a woman's porch. Even in my own apartment things were out of kilter, although I couldn't put my finger on what was wrong. Around the world armed conflicts were increasing, but many experts declared that it wasn't too late to set things right. Unable to cope with the world, I called Minni.

A sleepy voice came on.

"Yes?"

"Were you asleep?"

"What did you expect?"

"There was a lot of thunder."

"I didn't hear a thing."

"It was very loud."

"Not around here."

"What were you dreaming about?"

She perked up. "My God, I had a hell of a dream! There was a large man dressed in white."

"A man?"

"Yes, a man, at least two and half meters tall, with white teeth."

"How did you see his teeth?"

"Why are you asking?"

"To see teeth is a sign of intimacy."

"How?"

"Teeth are usually hidden behind lips."

"He smiled."

"At you?"

"Yes."

"Why?"

"I don't know," Minni said. "He didn't talk, it was like a silent movie, see, before he appeared, nobody talked, and really, I can't remember if anyone else I saw mentioned the man. All I remember is him."

"Maybe he would have talked if I hadn't interrupted your dream."

"I doubt it."

"But why?"

"He smiled, then turned away."

"Did he look at someone else in the room?"

"I'm not sure if we were in a room or not."

"Could have been a yard?"

"Possibly."

"Did he have all his teeth?"

Minni, breathing heavily into the phone, said after a while, "Yes."

It was my turn to hesitate. Artemidorus claims, among other things, that the front teeth mean overt, but the side teeth, covert actions. If some of the teeth fall out, it means that your plans will come to nothing. Since all the man's teeth were present, I was obliged to go to Leningrad after all. I sighed.

"What are you sighing about?" asked Minni.

"I'm sad. I'm alone."

"So what happens now?"

"Come here."

"I can't."

"Why not? Is Lussi there?"

"Don't get angry. No, Lussi isn't here, but we're going to Pärnu in four hours."

"For how long?"

"A couple of days."

I pretended to be upset.

"All right. I'll take a trip too. Straight to hell, see?"

"Please come back."

"Do you care?"

"Yes. I'll come after I get back from Pärnu."

I heard a distant thunderclap.

"Did you hear that?"

"What?"

"Thunder."

"I didn't hear anything."

"You don't love me."

"If you say so. I believe what you tell me. Always."

"You love that giant with white teeth."

"If you say so."

"The giant who turns and looks away."

"If you say so."

IN THE PARK

That park has an unsavory reputation—not that anything bad has ever happened to me there. Walking along I heard shouting: Stand! Lay down! Stand! An old man was training his German shepherd. I was alone, no Minni, no hope.

A wild rose was blooming by the footpath, alone like me. I was its only admirer. Bees were buzzing around the petals, carrying pollen, circling, but one spotted me, bit me. Or, to use the proper word, *stung* me. (My book is riddled with errors.) To paraphrase Shakespeare's *Tempest*: *where the bee sucks, there suck I.* This insignificant event affected me like a moral imperative and in that park it came to me that one must not reject choice. Am I not a free man? Look, a bee chose to sting me. Now it dies, but it did what it wanted. No one has pushed me. The letter didn't put any pressure on me. It was just an invitation. To go, it seemed, would make more sense than not to go.

This is Saturday. If the late evening train hasn't been cancelled, I'll take it. If I find out it isn't running, then the world is just against me, and I can't do anything about it.

That damned bee stung me in the back of my neck.

I'll go to the club and spend my remaining hours there with my friends.

IN THE CLUB

N., comfortable in his armchair, took a long drag from his pipe and began to talk.

"Yesterday I happened to be watching a debate on TV over whether Estonia should be free or not. Those against liberation argued that the Estonians aren't used to a free society. The pros pointed out that only in a free society can one learn to be free. (Yes, I must go to Leningrad, I told myself while he spoke: should I choose Leningrad, I'll become freer by having made my free choice.) So, while I took in the debate, the unthinkable happened—my coffee cup, just a couple of meters away from me, on the table and full of coffee, exploded. Flying pieces hit the ceiling and the wallpaper. What did the explosion sound like? I'm not sure. Yes, it must have made a noise, but the incident was so unbelievable that I may not have noticed the sound of it. The low growl is still in my ears—the short, low growl of a tiger or a leopard. Then silence. I have no explanation. Now the room is all messy, the wall is smeared with coffee stains. I'd been thinking of changing the wallpaper for a while anyway, but the shops had no paper; by the time paper became available, they were out of glue; when I decided to boil my own glue, starch had disappeared, because the starch factories, due to the gas shortage, had no potatoes; and by the time starch reappeared, the wallpaper factory was bankrupt. So I called the supplier and was told that the wallpaper would be in tomorrow. I'll go again and take a look, but I expect to be told that the paper will be in the day after tomorrow."

N. rapped his pipe against the ashtray, emptying it.

"But the glue?" I asked.

"Someone I know has some glue," he laughed. "He brought it in from Romania."

"Is Romania open to us?" I was surprised. "It's been on the proscribed list for a long time."

"Proscribed for some, not for others. Soon you'll see."

N. wasn't being forthcoming, and I didn't care that much, so we dropped the matter.

I checked my watch.

Only six.

The train was scheduled to depart just before eleven. I bought my ticket from the stationmaster's wife, who was friends with an actor I happened to know.

"The same," I told the waiter.

GO EAST, YOUNG MAN

The train was rattling and rocking, I could hardly stand up. To prevent nausea, I closed my eyes. Minni, Minni, if only you knew how dangerous this journey is! Where will I end up? I opened my eyes to the flicker of the ceiling lights that followed the rhythm of the wheels. All I could see in the windows was me, of course—outside it was pitch dark. By now we should be passing the oil-shale district, and indeed, in the distance,

I could see the glow from a little mine fire. The last time I passed this way, a huge mine had been burning—the flames could be seen from very far away. Now there was only a black night, the last of July, with no sign of that old fire that had drawn people in from near and far to warm themselves and exchange glances, wondering what it all added up to. Now, in the distance, one pit still glowed, its pale fire illuminating a few crumpled iron pipes, a few burnt tree trunks. It faded, came again, sad, alone, without any firefighters—an abandoned site where only recently hope was still alive and energy being produced. This decaying fire-nest having slipped behind a forest, we rolled past the deserted platform of a small station out into another dark space. In this land hollowed out by shafts and tunnels, dead rats floated in oily water, but we didn't see them—the land was asleep on both sides of the tracks, and it was impossible to collect my thoughts, since I had a feeling that all my thoughts had already been consumed when I was young. How many word combinations are there, after all? I sat, staring glassily at nothing (like the character in that novel who's supposed to take one last look at the moon before it sets behind the high and empty mountains—Doderer).

But who's out in the passageway?

Something was moving behind the glass door leading to the exit.

I decided to investigate. Yes, something had appeared and then vanished. A paw was scratching the glass door. It belonged to a big black German shepherd that was panting and drooling and sticking out its red tongue. I didn't dare let the animal in—I had no idea who he belonged to and why he was there with nobody keeping an eye on him. Seeing me, the dog rose to his hind legs and began to bark.

The train rattled on. Most likely we were east of the border now. What should I do?

I staggered to the other end of the car and knocked on the conductor's door. No answer. I knocked again. The door slid opened a crack. A woman looked at me sadly. Her chin dripping with tomato juice. She was holding a glass.

(The following conversation was conducted in Russian.)

"What do you want?" she sighed.

"There's a dog on the train."

"What kind of a dog are you talking about?"

"Not sure, it's just a big black dog."

"Is it bothering you?"

"Not yet."

"Then, so what?"

"Whose dog is it?"

"Not mine."

"Does it have to be there?"

"No, but it is there, and I can't do anything about it now."

"But in the morning?"

"We'll see. Want some juice?"

"No."

"Too bad. It's good."

I noticed that her uniform was open in the front. Underneath she was naked. I'm by no means a prude, but I resent being harassed by flagrant sexual stimuli in the middle of the night with a perfect stranger on the way to Leningrad.

"Do up the buttons of your uniform, please."

"Does it bother you?"

"No. We were talking about the dog."

"I'm asking if my naked body bothers you."

"No, but . . ."

"Are you married?"

"Almost."

"What does that mean?"

"Don't know."

She opened the door wide and gave me a deep, reproachful look.

"What a son of a whore you are," she said, sounding sad. "Who's waiting for you in Peters? *To sto, stregoits ne boisja?* Go to hell. Sleep in peace."

I became stoic, and, ignoring the dog, returned to my compartment, which was reeking of garlic. I couldn't see my fellow travelers. I groped my way to an upper bunk and stretched out in my clothes. Someone snored. Some light from the passageway leaked in through a crack. The rattle of the train was putting me to sleep. A shadow appeared in the crack under the door. I heard sniffles. Evil spirits! Leave me alone! I must not give in to temptation. Let the limping donkey driver reach out for his stick that he dropped on the ground. Let the floating corpse raise a hand in supplication—I will pretend I have not seen or heard. The dog sniffs, gives up, sighs, goes to sleep. A dog bites you only when you bother it. When you lie down and keep still, he soon forgets you. Why not do some forgetting yourself? Forget who you are, forget that you've forgotten.

The train stops. I heard someone running in the corridor.

The train began to move again.

LENINGRAD

I'd left Tallinn July 29, half an hour before midnight, reaching Leningrad at 8:30 the next morning. My head ached. The West was no more—this was the East. During my wait at the club I'd drunk quite a bit, had finally mentioned my invitation, even asked my friends if I was doing the right thing by braving the unknown. No one bothered to respond to my problem. They only wanted an audience for their own problems. The man across the table from me had also received an invitation, but it was to a military commission. I listened to his concerns, but had little sympathy: At least he knew where he was going. A no-longer-young woman said that she herself had felt, at times, some undefined invitations, but this was much too abstract for us.

I have no friends in Leningrad. Long ago I had a few, but ties loosened, letters stopped. The present day Leningrad was a stranger.

I called on Dostoyevsky for a guide. Of course I already knew that this great stone city had been built on swamps and water. V. Odoevsky writes about an old Finn who tells us that "They began building the city, but no sooner was a stone set in place than the swamp swallowed it; stones were piled on top of stones, timber beams on timber beams, but the swamp sucked all of them down; only slime remained on the surface. The Czar built a ship, sailed out, looked around, and saw there was no city. 'You can't do anything right,' he told his servants, and having said this, began lifting stones one by one and fitting them into the air. He built the entire city this way, then lowered it to the ground." Thus, since the time of its creation, that city has been unreliable and phantasmal. Dostoyevsky: "Suppose that the fog lifts; doesn't the rotten, slimy city vanish along with it, dissipating like smoke, leaving behind the primal Finnish swamp?" But what good is all this knowledge when, on leaving the Warsaw Station in the early morning, half-expecting to be met by green-faced swamp creatures, you find that there's no snow falling, and that the people around you appear to be perfectly normal? It's summer and the sun is shining. You go along with the crowd—a little ill, a little healthy. The world on the street is so bright, you begin to suspect that you're in the wrong place, worry that your awkwardness in all this brightness is getting you unwanted attention. Unless everyone on the street—you can't be sure—is having similar ideas, the same worries and hopes?

I recalled how, in 1950, I visited Leningrad with Aunt Ida to buy sugar. Those were difficult war years and there was no sugar to be had in Estonia—just as now. In Leningrad you could buy it—I can't remember just how many kilos of sugar per person. That's why she took me along. My aunt told me to get in line twice. I felt ashamed. I was a country boy and thought that this was cheating; also, that I'd be found out. Then I had an idea—I'll scrunch up my face so that the saleswoman won't recognize me the second time. I lifted my upper lip under my nose as if I'd smelled something awful. Although the saleswoman was taken aback, she did give me another portion of sugar. Now I was in that same city again. Of course, in the meantime I'd been there a few times on business—twice to the Finnish Consulate and for something else as well. This time, however, I was looking forward to a secret meeting that could very well be—unless I was careful—the last meeting of my life.

Did I say that I got off the train at Warsaw Station? It was by the circular canal adjacent to the Baltic Rail Terminal.

I told the cabbie, "*Kreiser* Aurora, *pozaluista.*"

> Over there, across the black span
> Of the Nikolai cast-iron Bridge
> The deadly serious *Aurora* lifts its
> Broad-shouldered towers.
> —Vladimir Mayakovsky

THE SHIP

The *Aurora* was built in Petersburg in 1897—actually, that's just when the keel was laid. The ship was launched in 1900. She sailed to Port Arthur in the Pacific Ocean and took part in the unfortunate (for the Russians, that is) Battle of Tsushima, which even Lenin called a shameful affair. By 1906 she was back in the Baltic, in 1909 she sailed to the Mediterranean, and again in 1911. A year later she toured China and Java. From 1916 on she was in dry dock. I gleaned all this from *The Immortal Ship*, by Jevgeni Junga (a pen name?). Why did I bother to read such an obscure book? What else should I have read? My peers all grew up in urban environments, in literary families that had extensive libraries. A few had read Jules Verne before they were even ten. But I read about the *Aurora*—nothing to be ashamed of. The book is sprinkled with metaphors and nice, vivid descriptions, even if its intentions were questionable. Literature is literature, be it Hemingway, Flaubert, Lermontov, Junga, or Joyce. Take these excerpts from Junga: "The lock of the six-inch gun clicks darkly. Beyond Dvortsovõi Bridge, impenetrable fog hangs over the river." Is this not evocative? Perhaps not a meticulously drawn picture, but still: the night, Dvortsovõi Bridge, a dark click . . . Or how about this: "A roaring laughter echoes through the cabins and around the decks . . ." Or this: "Before he could end his story, a haymaker sends the Bosun's Mate crashing down on top of a stool by the toilet. With a single heave, a sailor empties his bucket full of stinging lye over the Bosun's head." Can you tell me these sketches aren't clear, that the action isn't intelligible? According to Roland Barthes, all good writing hides behind a mask while pointing a finger at its meaning. Doesn't Barthes's description fit Junga? In any case, I did enjoy reading Junga when I was a child. I even remember his description of how two delegates of the striking workers of the city—dignified, bewhiskered—had an argument with Ignatõts the Guard. He warned them not to go back home before dark, since the Officer in Charge would arrest them on the spot, and they would not be permitted to reboard the ship once they disembarked. The delegates thought it over. Ignatõts then added that the crews of the Czar's Navy would never side with the Masters. The upper classes were burying the truth, but now the sailors had their eyes open.

When I arrived at the *Aurora*'s dock, everything, of course, was different. There was no impenetrable fog to wrap itself around the upper stories of the city buildings or crawl under the arches of the bridges that span the frozen canals, to roll along the silent avenues or spread itself on the slimy granite banks of the Neva, Moika, and Fontanka. I did, however, see the wind sweep up dry dust, the hot sun beat on the gray flanks of the cruiser, and my cab leave in a hurry, abandoning me on the quay like an orphaned child.

The sun was overhead. Cars crawled in the distance but none came my way. I felt exposed on the quay, highly visible to invisible observers—perhaps they were weighing my strengths and weaknesses, checking my nerve. Or perhaps they were consulting among themselves as to how to approach me? The cruiser itself had three high smokestacks and two masts. In the old days, a man-o-war was also fitted out with sails, to be used if the winds were favorable. I lit a cigarette. It tasted foul. A few sparrows that landed nearby eyed me suspiciously. I stamped my foot, scaring them away. Perhaps I was a victim of a conspiracy, and my apartment was being ransacked that very moment—the KGB conducting a search, or maybe it was just being vandalized? Why didn't I tell Minni where I was going? She trusted me about her trip to Pärnu with Lussi. Minni could have kept an eye on my apartment, especially now that the burglary rate had increased by 92% in the last year. What did I have worth stealing? I had some souvenirs, I supposed, some dusty flowers of the past, which might fetch a few measly kopecks on the black market. Minni collects such things, as I had observed during our brief relationship. But what if this entire conspiracy was aimed at Minni and not myself? That would account for their wanting to get me out of the way, out onto the hot cobblestones by an old warship, under the guns of the Russian Revolution.

"Guten Tag," said a voice behind me. "Izvinite, sto opozdal." (Excuse me for being late.)

28

II

The collective unconscious of a species is vastly more powerful than any personal unconscious, and under appropriate conditions it can directly materialize a thought form, which may be a material object or even a living being.
—Thomas Bearden, Alabama physicist

MORE SYNCHRONIZED EVENTS

1

I only know this peasant casually, the peasant who was there that evening, who this happened to, yes was only *there,* since it's not easy to be sure if he actually did or didn't do anything. Things are still foggy, the way binoculars get when you bring them into a warm room from a January frost. This much we can be sure of: a peasant. I don't even know if he was a peasant before the Soviets, or if he'd only become a peasant recently. Let's assume that he gets up at dawn. He opens his bleary eyes and hears a dog barking. The peasant goes up to his window and pulls aside the curtain. The sky is blue and starlings are singing. It's the middle of summer. He scratches his back and coughs. Yes, the world is so pretty at dawn. But he has an odd feeling. Something appears to be wrong. He goes out to the yard, checks the barn, the woodpile—but nothing is out of place. He checks his watch: four o'clock. He realizes: there's too much light. And the sun, although clean and sober, is looking down from the wrong angle. By then the peasant—whose personal history and background we don't really know—begins to put two and two together. On the living room table is an empty bottle of vodka and an ashtray full of cigarette butts. Who was here? Kaarel? Yes, Kaarel. Then our peasant understands it's really afternoon. He'd begun drinking with his neighbor at midday and soon fell asleep. His sleep had been brief. He soon woke and looked around, thinking: dawn, farmwork, grass waiting to be cut. Yes, a mistake. Somehow he'd mistaken the sunset for the dawn. This can happen. But nothing has been lost. He goes back to bed, goes back to his sleep. The real dawn is still to come. He's been given an extension. Some extra time. This sleep he stole from life. Sleep until dawn, peasant. Sleep.

2

Our unknown peasant confused the time of day in July, 1986. That same month a woman in a Tallinn suburb heard what sounded like a knock on her front door. Could be a ghost, she thought, ignoring the knock. The knock sounded again. The woman, home alone, hesitated. It can't be anyone, she told herself. It's late. Her husband and children were off at grandma's and weren't due back for two days. And if it was them at the door, if they'd come back early, the knock wouldn't have been so tentative. Also, she would have heard her children yell, "Mother! Mother! Open up!" I don't want to open the door just to see an empty hallway lit by that fly-blown bulb. Why should I have to look at that? Another knock. A ghost wouldn't be so persistent. The woman, of course, could only assume this. Actually, she knew nothing about ghosts. Only what her mother had told her. But that was a long time ago. Her mother was dead now. Now the woman had to decide for herself. And, strangely enough, she did decide. She went to the door and opened it. The hall wasn't empty. A strange blond man was standing there, who asked if (. . .) was living there. Naturally not, the woman replied. Nothing natural about it, said the man. I was given this address, so I came. If there's some mistake, I'll excuse myself and leave. Can you can tell me where (. . .) might live? No, replied the woman, I've heard the name, that's all. The man hesitated a moment, bowed politely, and left. The woman closed the door. She began to knit. She'd never seen a ghost before in her life, and it seemed she still hadn't. That made her laugh. Earlier that day she'd eaten cabbage, which gave her a bloated feeling. Slowly the day waned. These older city suburbs could have been full of imposing white villas by the sea and the sounds of classical music, but instead? What do we get instead? Those working-class barracks, jerry-built after the war, will never know beauty —if by beauty we mean the classical order purity of style of traditional western art. Yes, that kind of beauty they'll never see. It's perfectly natural to assume that no one else knocked on the woman's door that evening, and that she went to sleep peacefully—assuming, of course, that she did eventually get to sleep.

3

Another young woman was busy cooking blood-mixed dumplings. She followed the recipe exactly: take three cups of blood
(her retired mother, who lived in a village, had just slaughtered
a pig), pour the blood through a sieve, add one and a half
glasses of milk, then fry cubes of pig fat together with onions,
and add ten cups of flour. That made dough that after a lot
of kneading could be shaped into dumplings. What then? She
boiled water, added salt and spices, dropped the dumplings in,
and simmered them for half an hour. Meanwhile she went to
the window and saw among other things that the trees outside
were about to drop their leaves, although it was unseasonably
early. As the dumplings boiled, they changed from deep red
to a lighter hue, and the young woman continued to stand
at the window waiting for her man to come home. She was
getting uneasy—another half an hour had passed, the dumplings were done, the pot was off the heat, was covered with
a towel, a bright white towel her grandmother had embroi-
dered, but her husband still wasn't home. To make a long story
short—for we must abandon this woman and take up another
theme—he never did come home, at least not that evening,
and perhaps not the following evening either. Yes, this woman
with the absurd dumplings she had cooked out of a sense of
obligation and not love, as if anticipating that the dumplings
would never bring happiness to anyone. Why the dumplings,
and why on that particular evening? Is there a hidden meaning
here? Did she want to tease, to challenge fate? Or was it a for-
lorn attempt to save this marriage of hers, begun only a year
ago and under doubtful circumstances? She could have chosen another man, the one who was in the army for instance, or

even a third one who lived nearby, but was extremely shy. In any case, she'd imagined a different, more interesting life for herself. Now she was standing at the window, and we'll never know what became of her.

4

In the middle of the night, Renner felt someone squeezing his hand. By the time he'd freed his hand, he was awake. Renner remembered everything, but strangely jumbled.

Yes, it was three o'clock, and three came after two, and if he was left alone—that is, if no one grabbed his hand again—the clock would soon strike four. In great detail Renner recalled Eurüüt asking Potaamia to dance; it was only much later that it became clear what this invitation was really for. At first, Potaamia, not understanding the gravity of the situation, replied to the Eurüüt's neighing with laughter, merry laughter that was almost a provocation . . . Did anyone understand what was going on? No, not a one: Eurüüt's white teeth and his quivering nostrils—it must have been a joke, certainly nothing serious. It was late in the evening, though still before sunset, a good omen for the wedding, but only Teese noticed how, a long way off a missile soared into the innocently blushing western sky. Meanwhile Eurüüt laughed and laughed, along with the rest of the wedding guests.

Renner closed his eyes, opened them again.

The clock meant something . . . but what?

5

Anderson stood by the showcase pretending to inspect the bottles on display, and nobody realized that he was using the glass of the case as a mirror to spy on the saleswoman and his customers behind him. Anderson himself didn't know when the decisive moment would be, and what he'd do when it came. He'd gone into the shop without a plan, hoping circumstances would be favorable. The shop was hot and Anderson sweated, but he was loath to leave the place empty-handed. The light on the street was razor sharp. The air had a peculiar innocence to it that crumbled one's will. When Anderson faced the showcase again, he spotted the saleswoman handing a customer a few rubles change. Anderson leaped to the counter, grabbed the notes out of the saleswoman's blunt fingers, and, slipping on the parquet floor, stormed out, the fresh air slapping at his face. He ran across the street, but before he could reach the far side, he heard a scream: Catch him! People being slow to react, Anderson gained another twenty meters or so. By now the saleswoman was screaming at the door of her shop. Anderson glanced over his shoulder. Two men were after him. Anderson cut a diagonal path across the street, but a man with a felt hat and a briefcase extended a leg, tripping him, and Anderson found himself face down on the tarmac. As he slid, the rough surface scraped some skin off his face. Blood ran down his cheek into his mouth. Trying to stand, Anderson was kicked in the neck with a sharp-toed boot and he blacked out. A Black Maria took Anderson away.

That happened in Kaunas in 1980. A few years earlier I'd visited Jonas in Lithuania. He was getting ready to immigrate to the United States. Our thoughts were gloomy. Would we ever meet again? My friend wasn't all that sure about his plans. The government had thrown all sorts of roadblocks in his way and he'd been fired from his job. We went for a walk; in a sculptor's atelier we took a look at some wooden images of Christ and other allegorical works. When night came, we were in a taxi, riding through the woods. It was raining hard. Our headlights caught an apparition madly waving his arms, his jacket spattered with blood.

"What do you want?" our driver yelled.

"Switch on your dome light," our "highwayman" ordered.

"What for?"

"I want to see who's in the car."

"What right do you have to order me around?"

"I have the right."

"Show me your papers, then."

The man took something out of his pocket, but stayed a considerable distance away.

"Come closer," our driver suggested.

"Can't you see?"

"I can't see a thing."

"I insist you do what I say." The man was resolute.

Our driver lost his temper. "You know what, kid—climb in and take the back seat. I'll take you to the station and we'll find out who you really are."

The man shook his head.

"Come on, let's go!"

Our "hijacker" turned and vanished into the rain.

We arrived at the hotel without any further adventures. The next morning the train took us out of Lithuania. I did visit that part of the world a couple more times, but lately haven't had any reason to go there.

I mention these two events because—for some reason they came to me on the day I completed my novel. Apparently they belong together. A writer has to be realistic!

6

This much we know: In those days the city bureaucrats were expected to head out to the collective farms to lend a hand with haymaking. Many offices closed their doors during the haymaking season. We can only guess what the rationale was for this, maybe they'll tell us one of these days, but for now let's just accept that that's how it was.

They sang on the bus ride out:

> Where the pavement stops, you wait,
> Your heart will tremble if I'm late.
> Between us the miles are long and stark,
> Between us are poverty and work.

I like to dwell on these people. They give out a kind of joie de vivre, or something.

The bus stopped at the farm's office.

At the first glance the surrounding buildings betrayed nothing at all unusual, neither wealth nor poverty.

The city folks spilled out, stretching and rearranging their clothes.

The foreman met them with a broad smile.

Some eager ones wanted to start immediately. Their hands were itching for work. The foreman said that it was too late for that today. First freshen up and scrub away the travel dust. This suggestion met with approval. Someone even clapped. It seemed that anything the foreman said would be received with good cheer. The crowd happily followed the foreman out of the courtyard. Some ladies called that they wanted to get their things off the bus, but others called back that there would be plenty of time for that later. After some confusion it was decided that they'd leave their gear on the bus. All this time the foreman stood patiently at the gate. Then he resumed his tour. One woman wanted them all to belt out more songs, but they hissed at her to cut it out: be quiet, look, the moon is in the sky. The country air was certainly much purer than the air in the city. They all noticed that. On their left there were some ruins. The foreman explained that it was a country manor that had burned down during the war. German troops had billeted at the manor; they were attacked at night by a Red Army unit, and in the ensuing battle the manor caught fire. This story sounded familiar, and quite a few of the city folks ventured to say that they'd heard it before. The foreman agreed: yes, this story is well known. Beyond a bend in the trail a dam and a brand-new reservoir could be seen. Its banks were grassless and bare. Clothes came off in a hurry, and soon the city folks were splashing in the water. The moon gave the scene a mystical aura. The visitors screeched and hooted, they mingled with the locals and soon it was impossible to tell them apart. The foreman was a dark silhouette on the bank. Was he moved by this sight? And why shouldn't he be? Wasn't it his initiative that had created that body of water? Someone declared that city life was nothing but garbage. She would stay here. Many agreed.

The next day I meet the city folk moving bales of hay to the barn. The work proceeds quietly, no more singing, people are busy with their own thoughts. Suddenly there's a clamor of chickens and humans. Work falters but no one knows what's happening. At the barn door a crying woman appears. Come! she calls. Help me! A fox has carried away four chickens, together with four cubs—she means to say that the fox had four cubs with it, and it had taught them how to catch chickens. Now three, no four, of her chickens are missing. The hay loaders are ready to give whatever help they can—even more, considering how distraught the woman is. They leave the barn. There's an old dilapidated farmhouse near the woods. That's where the fox and her cubs came from, the woman explains. She'd charged at the fox and screamed, but the animal just ignored her. She points at some feathers on the ground by the animal's escape route. A worldly wise man says that there's no way they'll catch the thief, but the woman laments that her legs are weak and the fox will come back and carry away the rest of her birds. On someone's suggestion a search of the forest is initiated. They find a deep and steep vale hidden in the woods. Suddenly they are breast deep in the nettles and alder saplings. Women yell that the nettles sting but no one gives up the search. A feather is found on the ground—the finder becomes their guide. Looking back, there is only forest. Any snakes here? No one knows. They climb over fallen tree trunks and push aside saplings. Hair gets tangled, arms get scratched, thorns reach for their eyes and mouths. Some worry about leeches. Mosquitoes bite them. By now their guide has dropped the feather. The nettles stand up behind them and they can't see where they came from. A panicky woman shouts that they're lost. Don't yell, they admonish her.

You'll scare the fox away. Isn't that exactly what this mission is about, someone asks? But, wait! What was that? Sounded like a chicken. They listen in dead silence. No, nothing. By now they're up to their necks in flora. Rustles all around, everyone panting, no way to know where they are. At last someone notices that to the right it's getting brighter. True enough, some sky can be seen between the trees. They emerge from the woods directly in front of their own barn. How did that happen? A wise fellow pontificates that since human beings have one leg that's stronger than the other, lacking a focus, they tend to walk around in circles. They all get back to work. One of the searchers feels sorry for the old chicken woman who got no help. Another makes a weak joke.

7

In Lasnamäe, where I live, the limestone has preserved some traces of a meteorite strike. The continental ice shelf rubbed the area pretty smooth, but they're still visible. The meteorite collided with Earth at an angle of 18 degrees and 08 minutes some 25,000 years ago, before the last ice age covered Northern Estonia. It was only after the ice melted—which took some 15,000 years—that it was possible to populate this part of the world. At the present moment the municipal powers-that-be are digging a canal for a tramway there. However, I hear that a young lady named Alli has planted herself by the meteorite site, declaring that she won't move, daring them to run her over with a bulldozer. She certainly got the attention of the dozer drivers. Is she for real? Who would risk their life for a crummy old meteorite? Of course, this young lady is indeed for real, and I admire her. I couldn't have done what she has done. To start with, I'm too much of a coward, and secondly, her tactics would be, for me, much too pathetic. In any case, I'm proud that little Estonia can produce such a Joan of Arc. To elaborate, the name of one of the bulldozer drivers was Walter, and I suspect that he's the one who that sad and previously devil-may-care wife was boiling those blood-dumplings for, was waiting for. All the circumstantial evidence at hand points to this conclusion.

8

Renner went out to the hallway, the blue shadows of the moon in front of him, behind, and on the walls. Having found the banister by touch, he hobbled down the stairs. At times he stopped and listened, but the house was asleep. On the ground floor he had to negotiate a corner. He counted doors: seven, two, five, three. He was after number three, the one with a black stain above the doorknob. He opened the door and stood listening. The moonlight didn't reach here. Somewhere in the darkness there was a potted plant—a geranium, a dwarf apple, or a wood sorrel. It's all the same to me, he thought. Renner sensed the presence of the plant with his body, and this elated him. Be whatever you are, Renner thought as he entered the ink-dark room. We know that the air smelled slightly of silver chloride and hydroquinone. Renner recognized these odors, even if he didn't know the names of these chemicals. He found the red light and switched it on. My nose works, Renner thought. There's nothing wrong with my sense of smell.

He'd come to this darkroom secretly. Not that it had been declared off limits for him, but he preferred to find his own way. Conspiracy is a drug. Like pretending to be a spy. To make enlargements in a darkroom secretly—is there anything that can lift a man's spirits more? A man who for years had been unjustly deprived of the life he craved? Three o'clock at night in the light of the harvest moon. He dipped his fingers in the pan and sniffed. It was hyposulfite of soda—we could have told him as much, but a good sniff confirmed it.

Horses! Renner had photographed horses galloping on the meadow behind the asylum. Tonight he planned to make copies of as many horses as he could, fifty at least. He put the paper under the projector and switched it on. How many seconds? Tell me! Help me! How long? He doused the light. The paper came out black. Overexposed. Heart racing, he tried again. He counted his heartbeats, dipped the paper in the solution. For a few seconds nothing happened. Huge trees rustled around the house, the old park was full of lost souls and tender memories. Under the bushes small creatures were curled up, and high on the tree branches too, birds were puffing up their feathers, all trying to keep warm. During the summer? Yes, even during the summer. The picture began to develop. Renner sloshed it around in the bath with tweezers.

A horse.

Renner snorted, looked around—nobody had heard him.

He began to laugh.

Now he really remembered everything.

Röötus had jumped up, grabbed a burning tree branch, and hit Karaks on the head. The next moment Karaks's hair began to burn and the blood flowed from his wound, hissing like an iron bar dunked in cold water. Röötus stood on his toes to better take in the amazing scene. Karaks, burning and bleeding, would not surrender. He picked up a timber beam and swung it at Röötus. But Karaks, blinded by his blood, miscalculated. His swing missed Röötus and hit his own man Koomutus, who dropped as though he'd been mowed down by a scythe, and no one could remember what he yelled before he died. Röötus hopped around on his back legs and neighed like a foal. He chewed through the Koorutus's larynx, then thrust a flaming torch down Euaager's throat, who choked, smoke spouting between his bloody teeth. But Röötus had overplayed his hand. A moment later, as he was coming up behind Trüüat, someone planted a pole-ax in his shoulder, near the neck. Amazingly, the wound wasn't fatal, and Röötus escaped out into the field, running through clouds of dust, screaming and yelling who knows what. The dust and blood on him congealing into paste, Röötus kept on running away from the battle and the war. Half-blinded, the rest of them also ran, everyone by himself, not recognizing one another: Ernes, Lugapass, Mörmar, Pisi-Noor, Voolus, Habas, Taum, and others. They ran, ran through the dust, the midday sun, everyone in his own direction, alone, some north, some north-east, some northwest.

Something moved, something was happening.

Renner tucked his enlargement under his pajamas and listened. Yes, it was out in the yard, barely noticeable. Wiping sweat from his eyes, he spread the blinds. Bright moonlight lit the lawn. Yes, it was coming nearer. Out of the lawn, silently, a conical mound of soil was growing. It was HIM. Yes, just him. What a terrible sight. Was he after Renner? Or had he come up through the lawn and the Earth's crust for no good reason, since THEY don't need a reason to do what they do? He'd better disappear. Tomorrow night might be more peaceful . . . Renner snuck out of the darkroom, the wet print sticking to his bare skin. He would dry it later.

9

Mikhail Gorbachov was touring the Far East. On a Vladivostok street he even talked with some ordinary people, according to a news report. MG asked: What impression do you people have of commerce here? It's good, replied G. I. Minejeva sincerely, a mother of three children. I bought all I wanted. We have a wide choice and the service is prompt. MG: How are the canned goods doing? The store manager K. V. Gorohhova replied: They're selling pretty well. Just now we have a new product on the shelves—sweet-berries in tomato sauce with vegetables, very popular. The next day MG flew to Khabarovsk and again met the people on the street. He said: You've been given lots of new privileges, don't you want any more? And a voice replied: No, that's enough for now.

The paper also reported on the Komissarov drama school students' production of *Hamlet*. Claudius was dressed up like a punk—or, rather, there were two Claudiuses, and two Hamlets as well. Frankly, counterculture does have its limits. I read somewhere that an American theater critic compared this radical *Hamlet* with a one-eyed black actress speaking her lines in Yiddish: It changes everything, the critic said. Another article in the paper dealt with the battle between the hot weather and the Temperance Society. No more beer will be sold on the beach at Pärnu, especially chilled beer.

> Hamlet: Tis now the very witching time of night,
> When churchyards yawn and hell itself breathes out
> Contagion to this world: now could I drink hot blood,
> And do such bitter business as the day
> Would quake to look on. (Act 3, Scene 2)

As an echo, a Tartu newspaper printed Andre Muller's essay "Hamlet without Secrets," where every word in the entire play is taken to be significant. This is understandable: All a critic has is the text. Dear God, what else could the poor man do?

The same paper published a demand for all rapists to be castrated.

That spring there was a nuclear catastrophe in Chernobyl.

One day I happened to see clouds of smoke accompanied by explosions over the city skyline from my apartment. Naturally, I didn't assume that a war had started. Feeling restless, I went out to the local grocery. (The shop was called Moskva, and near the shop there was an old man who we'll meet again later on.) I stood outside the shop, eyeing the cucumber and tomato vendors. From out of a thicket ran an Estonian warrior, a spear in one hand and shield in the other. His coat of mail was in tatters, and under its layers of sweat and dust, his expression was grim and sorrowful. Panting, he bought a jar of dilled cucumbers and began stuffing them in his mouth. People gathered around, especially women and children. I also stayed to watch.

This warrior swallowed a few marinated cucumbers, then began a monologue, mostly to himself, but at the same time to everyone around him, despite the fact that most of the onlookers couldn't understand Estonian.

"God damn it, the third time out it all turned to shit, they'll fire the cannon, no, and the wall will collapse, I'm telling you, the third time, a miracle they're still alive. I'm telling you straight, the fourth time will be the last, if the wall comes down again, I'm out of here. I'm telling you, I'll be gone. Gone."

In the woods a bugle blared.

The warrior flipped his hand in disgust and loped back to where he came from. I followed him. Under the trees the light was dim and gnats were thirsty for my blood.

In a clearing there was an enormous tank. They were shooting a movie, and the crew must have been on a break just then. Going closer, I could see that under the tank treads there was a girl in a folk costume. I'm not easy to shock—right away I understood that it was only a dummy. Nearby, the director was screaming at someone or other: "Are we going to get a car out here or not? We need blood immediately! And I'll tell you, if I see that berry juice again, I'll smack you! It has to be human blood! Where can we get it? How do I know! A hospital, a slaughterhouse . . . We're depicting the tragedy of the Estonian people, the turning point in our history . . . and you're fooling around. Our tiny country! Our terrible fate! Get me blood! And where are the occupiers? There? Why there?"

A bearded camera operator came along at a snail's pace announcing that they'd run out of film, and that the nearest supply was in the city.

The director moaned. "Days pass, life and time pass, and what do we do? We sleep."

He waved them away in disgust and sat down.

I went back to the gnat-infested woods.

All this happened a month before *Hamlet*, a month before Gorbachov's Far-East jaunt and the call to castrate all rapists.

10

Renner ate some chocolate, wiped the brown muck off his fingers, and took another look at his horse. He heard their neighing, their longing for freedom . . . How Eurüüt had grabbed Potaamia, and how he whinnied! When did it happen? Did it happen at all? Who beside Renner would know? If a question has no answer, what's the point of asking? There was, yes, gunfire clearing the ground for attack, shrapnel whistling overhead . . . Hilltop 4 waited, waited, until the regiment rose like a single body, yelling out its war cry . . . Or did it happen some other way? Was Eurüüt a part of this war, was he a soldier? No, it couldn't have been like that. The hilltop had to be occupied by someone else. Lieutenant Sasha? Confusion everywhere. True, the world in its entirety can never be explained—and yet, what do we mean by explanation? If it just means a description, we'll make no progress, we'll stay ignorant. Objective descriptions of chaos are chaotic, at least at first glance—but if we really tried, this could be the first step out of the chaos . . . if only someone was interested in taking that step, if some of us might be in the mood to try.

Renner: Teese stormed between them, tearing Potaamia out of Eurüüt's arms. What did I do? I must have been frozen in surprise, in fear and outrage. I remember, I remember that I was—

48

(Renner was required to carry out daily memory exercises, and, this being one, Renner is remembering what happened to him . . .)

Renner: Eurüüt objected strenuously to this treatment. He attacked Teese, roaring. The wedding party took no notice, some were drunk, some singing out of tune. Meanwhile, some other guests began grabbing our women. Blabbering, whinnying, growling, scratching the ground with their hooves, but all with a single purpose in mind. The women began to scream. It looked like the end of the world. At least, what the end of the world was likely to look like. Maybe the end of the world has already happened, maybe even more than once. Only Teese still seemed to know what he was doing. He lifted a huge, almost human-sized vat filled with wine and heaved it in Eurüüt's face, whose brains then flowed, together with blood and wine, into the sand. Two brothers were screaming: Arms! To arms! And so it started. Aamik stole our holy relics, stuffed them in a bag, and hit our beloved Seladoole on the head with a heavy candelabrum. Her eyes popped out. Then Laatus killed Müükus with a table leg. Grüün seized the altar together with its burning candlestick and tossed it at Brot and Ori, killing them . . .

There was a hiatus.

Snow, pure white snow.

Renner opened his eyes.

Outside his room it was summer, the sun was bright. Renner approached the window.

Linden trees, chestnuts, a lone fir tree. High cirrus clouds with a few gaps for the sun to peek through. Behind these barred windows, one could imagine that the city outside had been abandoned.

The empty paths in the park are yearning for feet, Renner thought, and yet here I stand at the window, thinking, thinking intently, until—

Yes, until? Until a miracle is born.

How is a miracle born?

The way everything else is born, naturally, with considerable difficulty, but you live through it, in the end.

Am I going to give birth?

Renner didn't know.

He was a skeptic, and for a good reason. I've waited so long, waited and waited, but nothing ever happens. No birth.

He threw himself on his unmade bed, pressed his red-hot cheek against the cold pillow. Light is scary: under the light, nothing ever happens. And no one ever happens.

11

The way the old man saw it, he'd lived an honest life, not that everyone else agreed with him. But isn't this every man's tragedy: to live and strive to the best of his ability, and then hear someone ask: what for? How often has this happened?

One day the old man accidentally saw something in one of the empty lots around the grocery store in the brand-new Lasnamäe neighborhood. The name of the shop, at the intersection of many winding paths, was Moskva. Here and there, abandoned construction tools were rusting away. Young boys used them to play soldiers, especially guerillas being tortured by the Germans. And by that shop someone was yelling: Help me! People were staring down an uncovered drainage ditch, not knowing what to do. It was only to be expected! Hadn't the old man always told them that this open drain was an accident waiting to happen? Pushing through the throng of onlookers, he yelled: "God damn it! Didn't I tell you that this was going to happen?"

Down in the pit, in the mud, sat a man with a deep scratch on his face. The empty lots in this area were dotted with drains in unexpected places. Some time in the distant future, the next century perhaps, the city plans putting in avenues, courtyards, and public squares, but right now there were only open pits. The old man, well aware of the danger, had even written a letter to the editor, but nothing had been done.

Our old man called a worker from a nearby construction site to come with a ladder, and that was that. The man who had fallen wasn't seriously injured.

And that's how the old man passed his days. There was never a shortage of wrongs to be righted. Once he spotted a cab driving over a newly seeded lawn. The old man found a crowbar and confronted the driver.

The driver's name was Joosep. He was on his way from one place to another. On the back seat there were two children, not his own but his cousin's. They were amazed to see an old man coming at them with a raised crowbar.

"Don't mess up this lawn!" he was yelling asthmatically. At first the arrogant driver intended to ignore this threat, but the old man, rather than step aside, lofted the crowbar higher and advanced another step. The children, scared, began to shriek. The driver swore and backed up.

This old man also had a grandchild he sometimes escorted

around the town. But the location of his own children, the parents of this grandchild, were unknown—perhaps they were prisoners, or dead, or on an official mission to some foreign country.

12

When at a loss as to how to proceed, we consulted a passerby, who told us the following:

"Oh, what do I think? You know, it's my opinion that my opinions hardly matter. On the other hand, maybe they do? If you, sir, want to put stock in them, that's fine by me, but for myself, my own mind is made up. I'm quite objective about myself. At times I have no opinions at all. For example, I find politics quite boring. Recently one of our politicians went away for some reason and then was replaced by another one—it caused quite a stir, and to tell the truth, I was upset as well, but not for long. I wasn't really all that attached to the old politician, and neither have I become attached to the new one. Should I have been sad or happy? The old politician was often ambivalent. What I mean is, although he believed Estonia should be for the Estonians, he made no effort at all to back up his belief with deeds. You might say he was flexible and favored letting evolution take its course. His replacement seemed to share this attitude. Therefore, in a sense, I preferred both of them, and when I felt like criticizing one of them, the other one shared my displeasure as well. By the way, I'm not the only one in our neighborhood who thought this way—really, it's quite natural. Can anyone make a better offer, considering how cool and sunny this summer has been?

"So we have to talk about opinions? So be it. But let's keep it brief. Also, keep in mind I'm not an important person. This spices up our conversation. Normally, things get weighed and analyzed. Hardly anything happens by chance. But I prefer to be unimportant. Let's pretend I've met you on the beach, and . . . Oh, that doesn't suit you? What do you want to know?

"I understand.

"Yes, certainly.

"When?

"So, not that long ago, yes?

"Maybe he had a point. God knows what I would have done in his place. Naturally, we never know that before . . . But we can always imagine. And while I imagine, I feel. It's only natural, there are psychological reasons for this. I didn't know him, never got to know him. Haven't even seen a photo of him. What did people say about him?

"Sure.

"That too?

"Naturally.

"By the way, they said that sort of thing about a lot of them. And often. Who knows, maybe even about me, the unimportant person. We're defenseless. Everyone wants to sound off. Maybe that's how it was with him, too. But a human being is complex. I can't remember who said that, but if nobody did, I'll say it myself. In the second place . . . Yes, of course. But if a human being has only two or three peculiarities, or sides, so to speak—for example, if you have only two noteworthy qualities, one could be dormant and the other one suddenly pop out during a difficult situation. Let's elaborate: a man is as simple as a spade, but all of a sudden he can turn out to be as complex as a hammer. Everyone is shocked: a human being is an enigma. These things happen, that's what I—an unimportant person—always say.

"How?

"No, let's leave it alone.

"Yes, really.

"You can easily put me aside.

"Other people too.

"I tell you, you can put anyone aside. For as long or short a time as is necessary.

"Are humans guilty? Of course they are. We have documents to prove it. Photos too.

"You know, I'm unimportant, but I don't believe that nations have a subconscious. You do? Well, that's your business. I don't want to start an argument. But tell me, which nations are you thinking of? Estonians and Latvians? Latvians and Russians? Estonians and Germans? Estonians and Russians? Russians and Germans? So many collisions! As an incidental person I recommend that you assemble your own version like a jigsaw or a mosaic. You know what 'mosaic' means? No, I'm not thinking of church windows. Don't bother me with churches. For all you know I could be highly religious. What does it matter that many people aren't, these days? Are you saying that if you aren't religious, no one else should be religious either? Let's leave the churches alone. I beg you. Your themes don't fit together. I'm thinking of jigsaw puzzles, like for a child. No, I don't have a child of my own, but I do play games. Not games of chance. A jigsaw puzzle isn't a game of chance. Maybe for you but not for me.

"And why not?

"Namely the puzzle.

"From where? From my preschool days. My mother stole one of the pieces. It might not have been my mother, but no matter. I assembled the rest of it, finally. It was a picture of a rabbit. The rabbit was life-size, I mean human size, standing under an oak tree, with a basket of eggs in its hand. From the relative sizes of the tree and the rabbit, I could see that the rabbit was human size, a veritable monster. As I was putting the pieces together to make the rabbit, I noticed the tail was missing. It's possible that Malle, the girl next door, stole the tile, but I thought it was my mother.

"Why did I believe that? No idea. But that's what I did believe. Deliberately.

"A psychoanalyst might be able to figure it out, but that really doesn't interest me. Back to that rabbit with no horns, shit, I mean no tail, rabbits don't have horns, but by *mosaic,* I was hoping to demonstrate the truth of what I was saying. But, you see, every time you start to speak, your head gets full of garbage and you go on and on, and later you feel miserable, why the hell did I talk so much, but you see, once you start you can't stop. For example: after the rabbit incident, I remember a cow, not a jigsaw cow but one made out of fir cones . . . But now I'm really going to stop. All the best to you, till we meet again.

"You too.

"My God, not that!

"Yes, let's hope so."

13

The milk truck went under the crusher. The plan was for the driver to erase all the traces of the crime. Details of the conspiracy were unimportant, and it's just as well that only the inner circle knew what was going on. The steel press began to clatter, flattening the truck into a pancake. But the ordeal wasn't over. A shaky voice exclaimed, "Look! Milk is flowing down the gears!"

"Yes indeed," said another. "And the milk is turning red. It's mixed with blood."

"Human blood."

The first onlooker shook himself from head to toe, as if to free himself from something clinging to his skin.

Here the writer has played a trick on the reader: he's presented a hideous image secondhand. Rather than describing the bloody mixture directly, he cites the onlookers. In old Greek tragedies murders always happen offstage, and later an actor comes on to describe the action. Modern film directors sometimes use the same technique, not out of a desire to be discrete, but to make their movie more interesting. Here we were dealing with a film. The audience got up, left the room, and locked the door. The TV set, now blind, was left alone in an empty apartment.

III

On a faraway sandy shore
I loved two lovely maidens
Daylight dying on the skyline
They emerged from blood red waves.
—Hando Runnel

TAKING THE SUN

The plane flew far and high, trailing white vapor, a long way from the sandy beach where two maidens were enjoying the sun. Nearby, bulrushes rustled. The plane flew over the beach, over two naked maidens: Minni on her back, Lussi on her stomach. The plane vanished into the blue, leaving behind the rustling bulrushes and the light peeking through the eyelids of the maidens. It all began with that metal airplane in the sky, created, as we all know, by Satan, and we could if we liked speak about its engine, about all its complicated mechanisms, its metaphysics, its vibrations, but by now the plane is gone, and the eyes of the maidens are shut.

They were silent, since during all the years they'd known

each other, they'd already had many chances to talk, and the lapping of the waves made them sleepy.

An hour passed.

Suddenly the enervating murmur of nature was interrupted by a howl coming out of the bulrushes. The girls sat up in a hurry and covered themselves. They couldn't see anyone. All the reeds looked the same.

"What was that?" whispered Minni.

Lussi shrugged.

No animal in Estonia made that kind of noise. It was more like an escapee from some tropical zoo, or a human trying to imitate an animal.

"We'd better get dressed," Lussi decided.

With their backs to the sea and eyes in the reeds, they dressed in a hurry and gathered up their things. The yellow sea of reeds hid who knows what secrets. Did they see an eye, an arm, a tail, or a yellow mane? Perhaps—but at the next moment, it was gone.

As they hurried towards the town, no head sprang out of the reeds to watch them go.

Had the girls seen a ghost? Was it a wounded bull moose, or an alcoholic exhibitionist who went back to sleep after one provocative roar? Was it a landslide behind the dunes? Was it some thug murdering a victim? A madman discovering his alter ego? Someone from the hinterlands seeing the sea for the first time? We could go on like this forever.

The girls, walking where the sea met the land, looked over their shoulders from time to time, but the beach remained empty.

"We were lucky to get away with our lives," Lussi said.

Minni nodded.

The smokestacks of the spa were just beyond the trees. Or, to be precise: one tall stack. Music was in the air, the music of summer; a high woman's voice wafted in the breeze. Summer, the wanton summer was here.

A young man on a bicycle, shirt around his hips, was riding on the shore in the opposite direction. The girls had no time to see if he had a mustache or beard. Barely past the girls, he looked back at them and tumbled into the water. He was clearly chagrined. How proudly he had approached them! And now he was up to his arms in water, trying not to curse aloud, trying to ignore the pain in his wrist. The girls, pretending they'd seen nothing, spared his manly pride. He had trouble getting up—his bike was still on top of him, but the girls left him to fight it out alone. Finally he managed to right himself, and pedaling like a madman, he aimed the bike at the headland. My friend, fly like a wind, disappear from our maidens' lives!

The girls were hungry and their nostrils took in the odors of soup, sweat, and unidentified white flowers.

"He could have been a gorilla like King Kong," Minni said.

"Do you like him?"

"Who?"

"King Kong?"

"Yes, a lot. I would have liked to sit on his lap. I mean, when I was young."

"I dreamed of a doctor," said Lussi.

"What kind of doctor?"

"When I was much younger. That he would touch me."

"Did a doctor touch you?" asked Minni.

Lussi shook her head.

"Then you must have been a strong, healthy girl."

Lussi nodded.

A LUNCHTIME CONVERSATION

Lussi and Minni, in an al fresco restaurant, were listening to the sounds of distant music, not the usual pop or sentimental schmaltz but patriotic songs frowned on by the authorities. "Why play this stuff here?" Lussi asked Minni, but Minni had no idea. A scholarly looking older man seated nearby, about to demolish his dessert, chuckled.

"My dear young ladies, don't you know that today is the day we honor the great Estonian poet Lydia Koidula? Many people, myself included, will be gathering at her monument. You being true patriots, of course, I'll certainly see you there. Come and lower your eyes in the memory of our first great poetess. You've heard of her, of course?"

The young ladies nodded in unison.

"I doubt if you know much about her," sighed the man, who appeared to be a teacher. "During these dreary and amnesiac times our educational system has degenerated quickly and I expect your knowledge will be superficial at best. We can't really demand of two future Estonian mothers—and mothers you will be, don't even try to dispute the point, for our first priority must be to preserve our population—but to continue, we can't really demand detailed knowledge about Koidula from our future mothers. You may know, however, that she lived from 1843 to 1886, and that her first collection,

Meadow Flowers, was published in 1866, being mostly translations from the German. I've heard it said that since Baudelaire had already published his highly sophisticated *Les Fleurs du Mal* a few years earlier, Koidula's collection was no big deal. My dear ladies, that's entirely beside the point. Every culture lives its own life. For us, Koidula is the symbol of our national awakening, no matter that this awakening came via the Baltic Germans and various other Estophiles. It appears that the Baltic Germans sowed fertile seeds . . . What are you doing?"

A surly waitress had grabbed the speaker's plate and dumped it in her cart.

"Give it back! I wasn't finished!"

The waitress either didn't hear him, didn't understand him, or just didn't give a damn—she carted the things away.

Our maybe-teacher smiled sadly and flipped his hand in disgust.

"So be it. It's not worth arguing about. Let's go back to Koidula. She married a gynecologist in 1877 and they settled in Kronstadt, an island near the present-day Leningrad. Just why did she marry that man? It's a mystery. You know what, maybe Lydia really loved him. I've also loved a woman considered by my acquaintances to be altogether unsuitable for me. Love is a mystery—but perhaps you know that better than I do. No point in spending much time on Koidula's marriage: we'll never know the truth. It's more important that we have her poems to appreciate. From the present day perspective they may seem a bit naïve, but we understand her intentions, and we must respect them. Here's an example: 'I want to hold you dear till I die, the blossom-filled country lanes of Estonia, the smelly land of my fathers.' You should know that in those days 'smelly' meant fragrant or aromatic. Nowadays 'smelly' means to stink. Things like that twist the meaning, but not so much that it ruins the poem. I'm a lot more interested in a different issue entirely."

Minni and Lussi listened with interest.

"One of Koidula's daughters seems to have been a tutor in Florence after the Second World War; she died there, but the site of her grave is lost to us. In European countries graves are important, have always been important, and yet we don't know anything about the grave of Koidula's daughter. Shame on us! Not one of us could be bothered to find her final resting place. I would gladly go and search for it, but would I be permitted to travel abroad on such a flimsy pretext? I'm not known as a Koidula scholar. I just love her, that's all. Did you young ladies already know the peculiar story of her daughter?"

The young ladies shook their heads.

"I'm surprised you know this little about Koidula. She wrote 'My Homeland Is My Love,' the traditional finale to our national songfests—even during the years when the song was forbidden. It wasn't actually forbidden, but it wasn't permitted either. Just like most things. As you well know. Her real name, by the way, was Jannsen—this was her father's name. He was a newspaper editor. But his daughter changed her name to Koidula, meaning 'dawn singer.' It appears she believed herself to be a Dawn Goddess, *Aurora* in Latin, just like the Russian cruiser that fired on the Winter Palace, beginning the new era. That much I'm sure you know. Yes?"

That teacher or whoever he was rose and cleaned his place himself, since the waitress was gone. Having done so, he asked, "Well, girls, shall we go?"

Lussi lied: "We need to make a phone call first."

The man smiled and took off in the direction of the music.

Minni was baffled. "Who are we supposed to call?"

"I just didn't want him around. He might have tried to come on to us."

Minni wasn't convinced. "He's old, and he looked respectable."

"Those are the worst. Didn't you notice how much he talked? That tells you a lot."

Minni yielded to the superior knowledge of her more sophisticated friend.

Still, they decided, out of curiosity, to attend the Koidula ceremony anyway.

THE MONUMENT

Lydia! You're now a stone monument with a lyre in your hand.

The sun is shining.

Minni and Lussi join the crowd around the monument.

Their hungers sated, they have a bad taste in their mouths.

A car stops on the tree-lined avenue, and a man comes out stretching his arms.

The crowd waves banners with slogans on them. Lydia gazes down at them icily, fingering her lyre. If you touch her on her shady side, your fingers feel the cold. Lydia doesn't warm up before August, but by then the short northern summer is over and the first leaves are falling.

So, this man got out of his car. Let's call him MAN—he

does have a name, of course, but MAN sounds mysterious, more threatening, more symbolic. I don't propose to describe how he looked.

So, the MAN exits his car on the avenue, and stretches.

Minni and Lussi are on the other side of Lydia.

RECAP

Once begun, it's vital not to lose the thread of the story, since once you lose it it's extremely difficult to find again. So, let's remember, all this began on a deserted beach not far from a seaside resort that's a thinly disguised version of Pärnu. Two pretty maidens, Minni and Lussi, sunning themselves on the beach, were scared out of their wits by a loud and threatening roar coming out of the bulrushes. They hurried to town and ate lunch at a self-service cafeteria. At the same time, a memorial public service to celebrate Lydia Koidula's birthday was being held at her monument nearby, and this service was attended by—among others—a MAN who'd came from the north, meaning the city of Tallinn.

All this happened in the second half of July, 1986.

AN INCIDENTAL EVENT

To begin with, an actress read the following lines from two of Lydia's poems:

Until I die I wish
To hold dear the

Blossoming paths
Of my smelly homeland.

And:

Your sons brave and strong
Your daughters in bloom
Like the prettiest of flowers
In my native country fields.

During her presentation the crowd was able to hear some discordant noises from the shrubbery, but at first no one paid attention.

A rowdy gang of youths was chanting: "Koidula! Freedom! Koidula! Freedom!"

Military men, pricking up their ears and eyes, got out of their cars.

Uncontainable forces, overlooked in the militia handbook, had been set loose at the celebration.

A woman dashed onto the square and tried to dislodge the actress from her podium by force. It was clear to everyone watching that the stone Koidula, the actress, and this newcomer looked rather similar, but only the monument kept out of the fray. The audience was confused—who should they back in this fight, and why? Piercing howls now blanketed the square. The chanting youths clustered together and yelled with synchronized passion, Lydia! Lydia! Lydia! Minni and Lussi stood on their toes, but being so ill informed, they had trouble following the action. They knew enough Koidula to pass their high school finals, that's all. I tried to enlighten Minni, but she showed no interest. I couldn't blame her. I didn't care for Koidula's poetry either—her weird personality engaged my curiosity without emotionally involving me. Naturally Minni sensed my lack of enthusiasm. The rioting on the square left them curious but uninvolved as well. Neither had they bothered to pay the least attention—suspicious of the possibly selfish motives of the maybe-teacher—to the knowledge he had dispensed to them so sincerely at the cafeteria. Had I been there (you may remember I was in Leningrad), I could have set them straight.

Of course, having read the signs, you might conclude that when something is in the air, it's in the air everywhere, whether you want it or not. Events happen sequentially. What happens inside us also happens outside us and vice versa. Something, he/her, thing, it . . . We need a definition here, but at times it's almost impossible to apply names. Haven't you experienced this yourself? We might give a name to something, but do we know what hides under that name? We might say "rabbit" but don't really understand that the entity who's been making use of that name is actually *****. Which comes closer to reality? I suspect "*****," despite its not having long ears or much of anything at all. Sometimes I can go on for hours on end about things that have different names from what I want. Therefore, something is in the air—and many of us react accordingly. There are visible signs. (As Jung says of UFOs: es wird etwas gesehen, Etwas!)

That summer, Koidula's reincarnation began to get noticed by more and more people.

If you expect me to describe this reincarnation of hers in detail, forget it. I'd be happy to talk about reincarnation, but the gist of our story has to remain shadowy, the way the Horsehead Nebula in Orion remains hidden behind dark interstellar clouds. This foggy metaphor helps me to escape having to define what, in practical terms, is a complete absurdity.

I'm not familiar with this woman. I lack the knowledge. I don't want some external, irrelevant force to influence me. Better that I stay silent. But I've inserted Koidula (true, after much heartache) into my novel, hoping that those readers who have been dissatisfied with the way the story's been going would find at least a few redeeming features in my treatment of her. I have done this much, and that's all I can do.

My God, I'm babbling again. So, anyway, the Koidula fans were screaming, Lydia! Lydia! Lydia! The actress who had been declaiming poetry was perfectly innocent of any malign intent towards the memory of Koidula, but the Reincarnation took her for an upstart, an imposter. Sure, the actress was good, but so was the Reincarnation. She had a good reason to be hostile to this actress, up there depleting Koidula's energy reserves. The Reincarnation couldn't exist on her own resources. She obtained them from elsewhere—the cosmos. The actress, sucking up the same energy in order to perform, was a danger to the Reincarnation. Thus there ensued an open conflict between two Koidulas. Stone Koidula, of course, remained indifferent. The noisy youngsters worshiped Koidula, but only their own image of her. They had arrived in a minibus, had patiently waited for the right moment, knowing that sooner or later a poetry reading would start up. When the usurper mounted the podium, the young people rushed in to stop her.

The actress, though taken aback, rose to the challenge.

Her eyes were burning like torches, like open fires, like glowworms, like flashlights—and then she received some unexpected help.

Two burly men in mufti approached the Reincarnation and grabbed her by the arms.

"May we help you?" one whispered in her ear.

"Let's go and rest," whispered the other one.

The Reincarnation hesitated but for a moment. Better to give in—a wise decision in most circumstances.

It's possible to win, but winners seldom evoke sympathy.

The Reincarnation whispered, "Let's just pretend that nothing happened."

The men agreed. They stepped aside and Koidula came down from her monument satisfied with her own transcendence. Aino Kallas in her monograph likens Koidula to a shooting star that appeared and then vanished like a snowflake in summer heat. This public appearance was her compensation for uncountable sleepless nights watching the golden dust motes dancing in her room; according to Leibniz, the soul is a creature's living mirror, when the lone wolf howls on the radio.

Koidula walked through the park, her dress sibilant.

One of her escorts opened their vehicle for her.

She sat down on the hot seat and closed her eyes. Her energy was spent.

For the moment, calm prevailed around the monument.

JOOSEP

Did I mention that just when our girls reached the gathering, a MAN appeared?

I'd almost forgotten him.

We're dealing with a shady character here, even bearing in mind that he came to give an official speech.

What about? Would it favor the poet? Fill the air with metaphors and oxymora? Not so. He began by speaking of the popularity of Koidula's books, and mentioning that she had been translated into many languages.

After these dry facts, the MAN went on.

If I keep on calling him MAN, he'll just get mixed up with other men. Let's give him a name. Let's call him Joosep. Why shouldn't he be a Joosep? It's a classy name: Josif would bring to mind Brodsky or Stalin, and José would be altogether unsuitable. And why split hairs: Joosep was his real name. Of course, sometimes it turns out that a particular name is unsuited for a particular work of literature. In that case, we'll change it. And not otherwise.

Joosep was between a rock and a hard place. He couldn't ignore Koidula's recent appearance. The audience expected to hear something stirring. On the other hand, his tooth was hurting like hell. He'd taken a pill, but it took time to work. With his aching tooth he spoke of Koidula's mission. What was her mission? Certainly patriotic. Her father was an educator in the broadest sense. At home they spoke German and wrote in German, but they disapproved of the Baltic Barons. Her brothers were drunks. One fell out of a window, the other one died of typhus. Not a suitable theme for a eulogy. It's not a good idea to cover up the truth—but, then, truth can be debilitating. The history of the Estonian people has many dismal and evil pages, but why dwell on the obvious? All our numerous invaders have made us a touchy people. We'd rather hear what's uplifting and good. Just like every other nation. "Our people are good" is a phrase that's dear to every heart.

Love of one's homeland—isn't that a positive feeling? That's what Joosep thought too. But the year 1986 wasn't ready for that kind of talk.

He spoke quietly and judiciously:

"It's not an exaggeration to say that, in our time, Koidula's poetry has found an echo in the Communist Party. And this is not an exaggeration. Some may disagree and look down their noses at me: go on, go on, how can there be a common thread between that poet of the dawn and the Party—despite the fact that communistic ideals were already germinating during Koidula's own lifetime, in Petersburg, near Kronstadt, where she lived? The echo, in any case, by no means obvious, is there nonetheless, and we should not be ashamed to speak of it, no matter what the dogmatists and the narrow-minded followers of Marx may think. Koidula sung her songs in a different era, and it's futile to search for communistic ideals in her poetry. No, we won't try to do that, and if this refusal puts a few more noses out of joint, so be it. But, her thoughts—her substance—I mean to say . . . no other literary work could possibly take the place of Koidula's. And right now, as we are about to assemble the 27th Congress of the Soviet Socialist Communist Party, which has been given the task of cleansing our society and accelerating the pace of progress, Koidula's artistic vision will aid us in ensuring the final victory of truth."

After a short cackle he continued:

"Despite our all-encompassing nationalistic cynicism, yes, despite our despicable sense of irony, let us not forget those who were instrumental in transferring Koidula's remains from Kronstadt to her native soil: Kaarel Idri, who found her grave, and especially Johannes Vares-Barbarus, Johannes Semper, Bruno Rennert, Eduard Pall, Nigol Andersen, and the many others who supported and actually performed the reinterment."

This would have been a good place to stop, but he was on a roll now:

"In the time to come, Koidula and her work will remain for us forever holy."

Finally he quit.

His head was spinning. The air was still. His armpits were dripping. So much talk, talk, talk—and for what? Who knows? A witch's circle can't be crossed. Joosep stepped down from the podium and sat under a tree in the park. Why doesn't anyone love me, he asked himself pityingly. Even Cornelia makes no effort to understand me. Not the slightest effort, although she must know what's going on in the world. It's all a dream, isn't it, the way the poets always say—Calderon, Grillparzer, our own Suits. It's all a daydream in the city, sitting in the central square. He stretched out on the cool grass. I can't stand Koidula, he said to himself. She was a loud mouth like me. Koidula, you stink! There are too many of you. I can't rationalize you. You couldn't even die the normal way. You waft through my hangover, fingernails untrimmed, the train of your dress covered in shit. Have you brushed your teeth, Koidula? Leave me alone—I can't deal with so many irregular hauntings. Koidula! The wounds still fester. Joosep turned on his side, pressed his face against the grass, against the soil. Even the soil reeked. Why must everything be so common, so natural—it makes me want to throw up. I no longer hope for purity and honesty. I don't want to hear birds chirping in their nests. Go away, water lilies. Give me vodka and smelly sewers, plastic countertops and neon lights. I want to follow the spirit of the times. Come spirit, come and save me from Koidula! What does the spirit of the times look like? Does it have wings? One face or many? Is it blind?

That's the way it is: even the best of us get caught, can be made sick, but this will pass in time. It happened to Joosep after his speech at the Koidula monument.

But he managed to control himself.

THE CRIME

Lussi and Minni were ambling towards the trees at the edge of the park. The sun was setting. A squirrel, showing its teeth, gave them a bloodthirsty stare before scampering up a tree. White butterflies bunched, swirled, dropped, soared, flew apart, repeated their maneuvers, and fluttered around the girls, who ignored them. Back on the square, the next orator began to spout—fortunately they were too far away now for his words to be understood.

Suddenly Lussi stopped.

"Look at this," she exclaimed, pointing to a minibus under the trees, its door open. Koidula was asleep on the front seat, a limp leg extended, a curl sticking to her sweaty brow. She was snoring gently. Her aides, most likely, had gone back to the festivities.

The girls approached the minivan.

Public appearances drained Koidula. Appearing at all drained her energy, but public displays were extremely debilitating. She usually slept for a full day and night after making one. She didn't dare consider another one for at least a week. Did our girls want to talk to Koidula? Hardly. They had nothing to ask her. Besides, they suspected she was an ersatz Koidula. There was a rumor going around that some sort of Koidula had appeared in Kohtla Järve too, but I don't want to get into that, the girls hadn't even heard that rumor. I had, but I was in Leningrad, and the rest of this story comes directly from Minni.

"We stood around for a minute or so. I didn't dare go any nearer. From where I stood I assumed that she was dead, but soon I could see and hear her breathing. It's weird that her companions would just leave her the way one leaves a pair of gloves in a taxi. They weren't her friends, I guess—they just made use of her aura. Lussi kept edging closer to the minibus. I tried to wave her away but she never looked back. Once that girl makes up her mind, there's no stopping her. Fortunately no one was around. In horror I saw that Lussi had already reached the blue—it was blue—minibus, and was extending her hand. Out of her mind! But I didn't dare make a peep. Then Lussi bent down to pick up something. She was back at my side almost at once, leading me away by the hand: Let's run! I had no idea what was going on, but I ran with her all the way to the bus terminal. Sitting on a bench away from the other people waiting, Lussi let me see what was in her hand. It was a signet ring!

"Did you pull it off her finger?" I asked, horrified.

"No, it was on the ground. Honest. Why shouldn't I take what she threw away? I don't believe she's the real thing. And I don't care for her poetry either. In any case, I have no regrets. Look! Isn't it exciting?"

"The ring had an L on a blue field."

"Your name's first letter . . . your initial, I mean."

Lussi nodded.

Buses came and went; the air was thick with gasoline fumes. A dog was running around aimlessly. The evening had come.

"I really don't know if you did the right thing," I said. Just in case. How could I support what she'd done?

She put the ring on her finger. It fit.

It was getting chilly. A wind came up.

We were going home.

LEAVING PÄRNU

Once in a while my cat Alma takes over my desk; then he starts acting spooky, staring off wide-eyed at nothing. Who knows—maybe he sees something in the foyer, an angular shape in dark clothes, an imposing collection of lines. According to the latest discoveries, profane materialism doesn't necessarily exclude other philosophies—although this would be too easy an explanation. My cat reminded me that Koidula once had a fleeting romance with the Finnish writer and linguist Antti Jalava-Almberg (1846-1909). A few years later Jalava married Alma, one of his students.

Meanwhile, Minni and Lussi are leaving Pärnu. Their money's run out. Also, Minni misses me and Lussi has a date with a young man and anyway the capital is just a more interesting place, where you're far more likely to meet someone worthwhile.

The road runs along a low hillside and is bathed in moonshine. The mist, white and opaque, apparently benign, on either side of the road, could however be hiding any number of ghostly creatures—barn-fire stokers, lucky eggs, bottom frogs. Still, the sky glows green and pure, empty of grasshoppers, birds, or other creatures of the devil, the way a summer night is supposed to be.

The girls were discussing some other things they'd heard at the Koidula celebration.

"What did *Mother's Day to be free of cars* mean?"

"The way I understand it, cars pollute the air, and it's children especially who get hurt by these chemicals," Minni said. "It was suggested that on Mother's Day we leave all our cars at home, so that at least on that day we can all breathe clean air."

"What's that got to do with Koidula?"

"Only that she advocated freedom for her people and air pollution is something that's been imposed on us by the invaders."

Lussi nodded. "It's so complicated," she said, with the moon reflecting in her enlarged pupils. "Everything's so tangled up, and to understand anything at all you have to separate things from each other, but then you try to think about how to put it all together again, and it all gets even more confusing."

"So don't think so much," Minni suggested.

"So what should I do instead?"

"Don't do anything, go to sleep."

"Lay down and sleep here on the road?"

"Yes. Go to sleep."

"Right now?"

"Why not?"

Lussi stretched out on the warm tarmac.

Minni squatted beside her.

"What now?"

Lussi sighed. "You know, a few young men are in love with me. I have to make a choice, because I feel . . ."

Minni interrupted her. "Sssh . . ."

She put her ear against the tarmac.

A FEARFUL CHILD

A five-year-old came down the road from the direction of Tallinn, walking barefoot and so softly that the girls didn't hear him. After he visited a friend, night had fallen while the boy was still walking home. Walking on tiptoes, he was listening to the grass rustling and imagining a ghost breathing down his neck. Naturally, it was a shock to see two still, bright shapes down the road. Two corpses? Were they bloody? The child ran back the way he came, and when he reached his friend's house, no words came, he just panted.

THE CAR

"Keep still," whispered Minni.

Lights were approaching.

Every suicide is familiar with this wait, whether it's on a

road, on the rails, or in a rye field in front of the steel blades of an approaching combine.

INDECISION

Every man with a career, more than halfway to retirement, knows what it means to have two bodies in his headlights. It's like two dragons start fighting inside his head, promoting two diametrically opposed courses of action: Help them quickly! one demands, they may still be alive! But the other one whispers urgently, Disappear, don't get mixed up in this. You may only be a witness, but the sense of a crime will be associated with you nonetheless. No one will remember what part you played, only that you were involved.

That's what Joosep, the featured speaker at the Koidula monument, was thinking.

THE JOURNEY BEGINS

He slammed on the brakes and got out. In any case, there wasn't enough room to drive around the figures on the ground. The headlights lit up two bright patches—one blue, one green. With Joosep standing there paralyzed, the girls held their breaths. The car's engine purred.

Lussi, unable to bear the tension any longer, burst out laughing.

The only thing to do was get up.

Minni waited for the man to offer her his arm to help her up.

"What time is it?"

"Half past eleven," the man replied.

"May we ask for a ride?" Lussi asked shyly.

"Sure." A curt reply.

"And where should we sit?"

The man pointed to the back seat.

Then he said: "Joosep."

The girls didn't introduce themselves.

THE ADVENTURES OF MINNI AND LUSSI IN THE NIGHT

The driver, silent at first, eventually became rather talkative. He quizzed the girls about their backgrounds, their jobs. The girls' brief but friendly replies seemed to satisfy him. He introduced himself again, but only by his first name. Nothing more. He didn't know how he should describe himself. He had an inconsistent history. A few examples: He'd saved three university students from being expelled on political grounds; he'd written an essay on the Tschukotka Peninsula; he'd vetoed the screening of Andrzej Wajda films in Estonia; had adopted a young black boy; had studied default logic in London for half a year; had been to Africa on a dangerous secret mission where he'd liquidated a new emigrant who'd become a nuisance; had demanded academic freedom for scientists; had written a few haikus. And he'd done all that from his heart, too, as natural extensions of his beliefs, and during some twenty years of such activities had remained as friendly and pure of heart as he'd started out being. Two years ago he'd lost his small son in a traffic accident. Now he was silently driving his car with two girls who knew nothing about him. On the passenger seat beside him was a black diplomatic briefcase that contained a study on the mentality of the younger generation, a bottle of cognac, and Orwell's *1984*—his favorite novel. There was some gray in his hair. The night was dark but not too dark. The woods were teeming with moose that refused to show themselves. His toothache was gone.

At the first glance, Joosep seems to be a caricature of a greater-than-life, or maybe a lesser-than-life character, though God only knows why I made him that way. In fact, his only enemy was language: the language this writer uses to make Joosep appear egg-shaped or prickly, and can do with him what it wants.

Accompanied by such doubts, the city approached—or, to be precise, the car approached the city. The TV tower became visible. Joosep announced matter-of-factly that he would take them all the way home. Minni and Lussi didn't protest. He seemed a polite and decent man.

The girls gave him Minni's address. Have I already mentioned that Minni's folks were out in the country helping out with the haymaking? They had participated in that failed fox hunt. Minni's mother was the one who'd pointed out that the noise they were making would scare away the fox. Did I mention that? I didn't? The ambiguous relationships among the characters in this story give me a headache. Their spider web of associations drives me insane. But anyway. Joosep took them to Minni's place.

Having stopped, Joosep declared that he wouldn't mind some coffee. Where could he get some? His tone was imploring. Minni, my true Minni, told him ironically to try a café, but happy-go-lucky Lussi suggested that they could all go in together and brew some coffee. Now it was Joosep's turn to be diffident—he really shouldn't, it was late, etc. In the end the girls had to beg him, and only then did Joosep lock his car and follow the girls indoors.

We must not fail to mention that old fighter for the truth, law, and honesty—he who had prevented a cab driver from driving over a lawn by menacing him with a crowbar, and of whose granddaughter we know nothing as yet, and who now stood in the corner of the courtyard of Minni's big apartment building. He practically lived right there in the courtyard. He'd liked Minni for some time, and her friend as well. He liked them and wished them well. Minni and Lussi could have been his daughters. And now, during his evening patrol, ready to take up arms against the prevailing chaos, he saw a middle-aged man in a dark suit toting a diplomatic briefcase. We won't eat you, he heard Minni's blonde friend say before the door banged shut behind them. This shook the old man. Surely it's an exaggeration to say that the old man's entire world collapsed, but something in him did indeed break. Let's not be frightened of grandiose phraseology. The old man leaned against the wall. It was too dark to see his tears—assuming he had any.

In the apartment, Joosep complimented the furniture and claimed a corner of the sofa. He suspected the girls were laughing at him. He asked, but the girls denied it. Joosep loosened his tie.

When the coffee appeared on the table, he spoke briefly

of content analysis, then gave up and said it's all nonsense, what's needed is humanity. He cradled his briefcase in his lap. After some hesitation he extracted the cognac and put it on the table.

The girls just sipped at it but Joosep really went to work on the bottle. Had he exercised some caution, things would have turned out differently.

Joosep declared that society was being reformed, but he himself had been demanding reform twenty years ago when the university students were clamoring for autonomy. But autonomy had been refused them. Who did that? GG, old GG himself, who else? Who else had the power to do that? Autonomy and GG were deadly enemies. GG hated the concept of autonomy. He was against any kind of national awakening. And now, in the year 1986, when the process is still incomplete, we can say outright that GG was an asshole. We can't say that about his buddies, or not yet, but pretty soon we'll be able to. Or maybe we won't, who knows, but in any case, we'll soon see. I hope we will. You don't know about GG? Jesus, I've hated people like you for twenty years, every one of you: don't be apolitical, be active! For twenty years I've told you bastards that everything depends on how you act. But did you listen? You said, "Why bother us with your Guevara, your Fanon! What do we care about Fanon? What are we, niggers?" That, more or less, was what your generation told me. I was right all along. Everything is connected. No man is an island. He's a part of a continent. Didn't I say that? But did I get any thanks? Now that our government is beginning to show a modicum of common sense, you can see that my actions were reasonable.

We've been rudely elbowed aside by the entire world, by Biafra, by Moscow, by the hippies, by everyone in every damned place. And what about you? Do you have any more cognac? Rubbing alcohol will do nicely, thank you girls. Yes, we're responsible for everyone. Sure, we've rebelled against injustice in Vietnam, Paris, Spain, and Kampuchea. So why not here? You have to realize that circumstances were unfavorable here. Politics is an extremely complicated subject. Our opposition was like a wall. It just wasn't possible to get through. But we are on the side of humanity, and must rebel against society's shortcomings. Dear young ladies, why didn't you support us? Damn your complaisant generation, that's what I would say, if you weren't so beautiful, the both of you. Yes. Yes. I don't lie. You didn't join us, didn't want the inconvenience of a revolution. And now . . . now you still don't want anything. Why don't you want anything? Did I want to make a speech today? No! But I did it, tasting vomit. It's necessary. Actually it's not. Do you have any records? Put something on. The Beatles, yes? Vysotsky! Music! Yes! Venice! What is this? Richard Clayderman, yes! *Italy, my love! O sole mio!* Let's dance. All right, I'll dance alone. Fellini, girls! I've been to Italy, more than once actually, but the night I was caught in the thunder and lightning on the Rialto Bridge! The Grand Canal was lit up one moment and inky dark the next, and you know, all of us who were there—the youth of the world, hiding from the rain in the lee of an old storehouse, all brothers and sisters, although it was difficult to believe, all of us pressed together . . . aah, still young . . . in love, *all you need is love.* In one of the prettiest cities in the world, in a thunderstorm . . . dreaming of a better world . . . of beauty . . . *my brother, my sister* . . . ah shit."

Joosep hid his face in his hands and staggered out of the living room into Minni's bedroom, slamming the door shut behind him. The frightened girls were frozen for some time.

Suddenly they came to their senses: what's that strange man doing in Minni's bedroom? Who's going to check on him? Who has the nerve? Lussi naturally. And gingerly Lussi cracked open the door. The room was unlit, but two eyes glowed in the darkness. Joosep was in Minni's bed, under a blanket.

He leered, "Welcome home, Little Red Riding Hood." Lussi was shocked, unable to speak, and so Joosep lifted up the blanket. He was naked. He let out a long howl. Without a hint of irony we can say that his howl contained all the radicalism of the sixties, and all its anguish too. Lussi escaped. No sooner had she reached Minni than Joosep came in on all fours, still naked. Bawling loudly, he mounted the ledge of an open window. Remember now that under the window stood the old man who was extremely fond of Minni and Lussi. He'd been standing there all night. And now, to add to his suffering, he saw a man, stark naked, imitating a pig and oinking into the night, perched on Minni's windowsill. An orgy! The old man had feared that something like this would happen, while still begging the fates to take pity and spare him. But the fates have no pity. Up in the apartment Joosep was screaming: Let's destroy this whore house! Minni, my dependable Minni, roared: Get out of here, pig! Joosep's oinking made her choice of words regrettably comical. He was pushed onto the stairwell, his clothes flying after him. Joosep threatened them, "Soon you'll go to the cold country!" but he was exhausted. As he descended the stairs, his faculties slowly returned to normal. He ran into the old man down on the ground floor, but they ignored each other. The cool morning air sobered him completely. He dressed in the courtyard. His car was gone, so he hailed a passing taxi. He'd been treated disrespectfully back in that brothel. As if he'd been guilty of—but fuck it, he was too tired to sort it all out. He jotted down Minni's address and phone number, intending to take his revenge. Then he merged with the new day.

The girls couldn't sleep. The scene they'd witnessed kept running through their heads. After barely an hour's sleep, Lussi went home. They promised to write each other if life got too boring in the meantime.

IV

Charon: One last request.
Namely, I'd like to see the vessels
Where their corpses are stacked . . .
—Lucianos

THE MEETING

"*Guten Tag*," I heard someone say, "*Izvinite, sto opodzal.*"

I turned around.

I hadn't heard him approaching.

We conversed in a German/Russian mixture.

"Eduard," he said, extending a hand that, considering the heat of the day, was refreshingly cool. "I'd heard the *Aurora* was docked here, and the place is widely known. Other popular spots, for example the Winter Palace and Hermitage, are crowded, as I've now seen with my own eyes, and here, I thought, we wouldn't be interrupted."

"Shall we go in?" I asked.

"Where?"

"The ship."

He laughed.

"Oh no, I said I selected this place for its visibility. Inside the ship I have no freedom to act and no power at all. In any case, the ship is closed to the public: see that rope across the gangway? No sign of life. Could be an off-day for visitors, or there could be repairs scheduled. Let's take a walk—here the sun will soften our brains and cloud our perceptions. Let's find a pleasant, shady park. Agreed?"

We went.

Now I could take a closer look at my new acquaintance. Blond, tall, with round, old-fashioned glasses. Moustache. Ashen face. Manicured hands. Age—fifty? Sixty? We walked side by side, silently. I asked, "You were certain I would come?"

"Not really, but from a certain perspective you had no choice. I presented my proposal in such a brief and persuasive way that it would have been difficult for you not to comply. Pleading and begging at length show a weakness the addressee will always spot, and then the proposal gets rejected. I apologize for being pushy, but I take pride in my self-confidence, which is usually rewarded. Mind you, in some critical circumstances my subjects have been known to act in unexpected ways. That is, if they see no alternative. Or if the alternative seems markedly inferior. In that case, one can be outspoken and go into detail. But tell me, have I ever bothered you before?"

"Never."

"You see. You see. And you'll live through this meeting as well. How does this bench look?"

Before I could sit he pulled me back by my arm.

"No, *Mein Herr*, this bench won't do. I was not being sincere. But you went along with me. You're an obliging person and that's exactly what I was hoping for. We'll take a cab."

"I'm not so sure we will," I muttered icily, to show him that my easy nature had its limits. He saw through my ploy. He laughed and threatened me with his finger.

"But *I'm* sure, because a cab is necessary. Look, here's one now." And he hailed the taxi.

As we took our seats I expected to hear him give an address, but he just sighed. "Am I correct in assuming you ate some garlic today?" he asked the driver.

It seemed to me that the driver blushed. He lowered his eyes and didn't say anything. "All right," my companion said, waving him away. "Shall we look for another cab?" The question was aimed at me. I shrugged.

"We'll stay. We'll put up with it," he decided for both of us.

He took an aerosol air-freshener from his pocket and sprayed around his nostrils and mouth.

I detected no smell of garlic.

"Do you have an allergy?" I asked.

He didn't answer me.

"*Na Petrusevskuju. Posle razumovskovo. Togda na Radzinskuju.*"

We drove through streets that were unfamiliar to me. Leningrad is a classical city and its architecture is consistent with the era of its construction. For a visitor, navigating it can be difficult.

IT'S GETTING DARK EARLY

"Getting dark already," sighed the man. "So what, we know the road, no fear of getting lost."

I looked out: true, the light was dim. Ever since that day I've wondered why I didn't react to that unnaturally early gloom. At the time I must have taken it for granted. We carry all sorts of received and parasitical information around with us. We remember from our early years, without ever having been to Leningrad, about the white nights of that city. Yes, white nights mean long evenings and nights as light as twilight. In strange and confusing situations, one tends to become desperate. It's demoralizing to think that it's only getting dark because your eyes are failing, for example. Better to think that the white nights are coming early, or to say, well, since the day was cloudy, the evening will also be darker than usual. I don't think I thought any of these things, or thought anything at all, if by thinking we mean a verbal text that's edited by the brain. I still keep on inserting and modifying such text, long after the fact, but at the time I felt only inevitability, inevitability evoked by the strange man beside me. I couldn't back out now, and he was so friendly that I was prepared to accept whatever happened. *Let darkness come. I'm not scared. If it's necessary, so be it.*

It's possible my memory is faulty. Today it all seems so much more sinister—but perhaps it really was only unusually cloudy. Perhaps we were dealing with a rare atmospheric phenomenon. I do recall a cloudy day in the winter of 1954 becoming violet, but no one made much of it at the time. Everything went back to normal afterwards and life went on.

One can speculate, doubt, and second-guess ad nauseam. Let's harden our hearts and trust our memory: I drove around Leningrad with a strange man, it was a summer afternoon and the light began to fade.

"Yes," the man sighed as to himself. "That's life: the road is familiar, no fear of getting lost."

THE RESTAURANT

By the time we were seated, it was dark outside. Or maybe not, since the curtains were drawn. At least I think they were. With those old-Russian-style restaurants you can never tell. Daylight seldom penetrates their dining rooms. A fountain gurgled. Candelabras glittered. You don't even think about daylight because you've entered a different world from the one you so recently inhabited, the world of brotherhood, equality, and God knows what else. No, we were now in the world of the Czars: here comes the waiter, the tablecloth is so white it shines, and look, a violin is being tuned up there on a podium.

Yes, that place had definitely been preserved from the time of the Czars. After we'd been seated I told my companion what I'd been thinking. He nodded:

"Yes, that's how it is. When the Czar was murdered, this country froze. And the love the Czar earned for himself during his life vanished entirely . . . I thought that the cat-o-nine-tails would be the best teacher for our people, a steel fist the most effective means . . . Iron and blood should have been the rule, that would have taught them. To think that creatures like

Sophie Perovska, the daughter of a former minister, found a place among our leaders . . . But forgive me, I became distracted, I got on my hobbyhorse. What shall we order? *Estouffade ou stockfish à la niçoise?*"

"I don't eat fish, excuse me." I felt more diffident than the occasion called for: when I'm in that kind of mood, I tend to draw attention to my odd tastes, and did so now.

"May I ask why?"

I searched for a sensible answer.

"I don't know, after the war, in those difficult times . . . I suddenly felt nauseated by fish . . . Once I vomited after eating fried fish, for no good reason, and then a reflex just developed in me, a reaction against it . . . something like that . . ."

Eduard nodded sympathetically. "Nothing to be ashamed of."

I also nodded.

"How about *cul de veau à la mode du vieux presbytère?*"

I nodded again.

"And *Wiener Obstpianne?*"

I kept on nodding.

"And from the wine list I'd recommend the Dauzac Margaux 1981."

"A Bordeaux?"

"Yes, from the Margaux district."

"My God, it must be expensive."

"You'd prefer something else?"

"How about a Castel del Monte . . ."

"No, look here . . ."

"No, I didn't mean to . . ."

"It's fine. Waiter!"

Of course, I wasn't paying—he had invited me. So why should I worry?

A red wine in any case.

By the way, Carl Gustav Jung's last words were, *Let's have a really good wine tonight.* He spoke in English because the nurse by his bed was from England.

THE WELL

Violins began to play, and the people around us transformed. My mind regressed to childhood. I'd certainly never moved in *cul de veau à la mode du vieux presbytère* circles; I knew nothing of restaurants, but I had had a radio and my own dreams, my own inner pictures derived from Estonian magazines with action stories in them that took place on great ocean liners, in saloons, and once on the Orient Express, accompanied by the *ratatat* of the train's wheels on the tracks.

I forgot I was in a strange town. I wished Minni could be there with me. Minni, come here, I can't follow what this man is saying. He's so polite, but I'd rather be listening to you, Minni. He's talking about how interested he is in Tallinn, in our lives, our struggles, defeats, problems, our history, especially the history of this last century. It all became so confusing near the end of the nineteenth century. There's no way I can cover it all in one evening in a restaurant. What can I say, Minni? Estonia is all I have. I was born there after the war, grew up in a grassy nook a long way from major roads—the only child of an accountant who worked at a creamery. There was a deep well, and my father forbade me from looking down into it. It had a windlass. It took three seconds for a stone to reach the bottom, and then the mirror on the bottom of the well began to ripple and I couldn't see myself in it anymore. Only after the waves settled—in that confined space, it took a while—did a tiny figure reappear at the end of that cement pipe at what seemed an astronomical distance. I understand it looked so tiny because the image had to go all the way down, then come back up to me. One day a water bucket broke loose—the handle began to whirl and the bucket dropped. While it fell, I felt an unbearable nausea, and then there was a crash and afterwards the bucket was as flat as a pancake. How can you describe all that to a stranger, Minni? The long mossy pipe of the well shaft, a blue sky at the end of it, Minni? Later an engine-driven pump was installed and it wasn't possible to look down the well, despite my father not being around anymore to forbid me. The water from that well produced an oily white scum when it was boiled. Would the man across the table from me be at all interested in all that, Minni? He claims that he's tried to keep up with all things Estonian, but news moves slowly, there's interference on the radio and all the maps are made up deliberately inaccurate, or so I hear, in order to confuse the enemy. My companion spoke of his desire to practice our language, because he wants to be fluent when he finally visits Estonia; he even claimed to be familiar with my writing, he'd read some of my books quite carefully, he said, especially my novel about Koidula— he'd read one strange novel, that is, and one play. He saluted me with the Dauzac that was dark as blood, and I remember that under our wine glasses, the tablecloth, despite the waiter's precautions, had developed dark red circles, and I also drank, and while drinking fell into a well right there in that brightly or dimly lit restaurant. I fell past sweating mossy walls, and at the bottom I saw a red rooster with a red comb and red wattles. This was the same rooster that gave the root of my nose an enormous peck, right below my right eye, when I was three years old and I'd squatted on the ground beside the bird. And now that rooster was at the end of this tunnel, waiting, beak wide open as though on a hot day, but instead I felt certain he was singing a song with the voice of a violin, a song that's sung on autum evenings in the suburbs, when one is tired of politics, when the rafters have been raised, or school's been let out, and yes, the rooster was approaching, or, to be precise, I was approaching the rooster, Minni, and I'd already fallen not three but three hundred seconds, and it was more like floating than falling. I remember my host talking and eating *Wiener Obstpianne*, but the rooster kept on getting closer, now directing and correcting my flight, no more songs and violins, only terse and exacting orders such as: *To the right! More! Now hold it, right there!* By now the rooster was much too near. I closed my eyes, but I did hear the boat bump against the seawall.

THE ROOM

I came to under a glaring light in a windowless room. I had a headache. I tilted my head to see I was flat on the floor. There was no furniture. And yet, I felt cheerful and I could have kept on talking.

Talk?

Did I talk?

Who with and what about?

I sat up with a start.

After talking a lot, one tends to feel depressed.

Not this time. Even my headache was agreeable.

Agreeable, yes, but why was I alone?

Tentatively I called, Yoo-hoo!

There was no reply and my voice sounded odd to me.

Sometimes you wake up in a strange place. So what? Am I a baby who always has to wake up at home? Does it matter that I'm in a strange place? I wake up, take a look around, and go home when I'm good and ready.

So there!

My watch, that piece of shit, had stopped.

Electronic watches aren't supposed to stop like that.

Since my watch had stopped, it seemed logical to me at the time that my money might be gone as well. This thought didn't faze me, oddly enough. I must confess I whistled while probing my breast pocket.

My money was there.

So, now we could go on celebrating.

Actually, why did I have so much cash?

Did someone treat me? Give me a present?

Who?

Wasn't I with someone?

Recently.

A PRISONER

Suddenly it came to me that I was in Leningrad, a long way from home. I'd come here to meet someone. We went to a restaurant. Then a rooster crowed . . . no, a rooster smiled at me. And now I was in this windowless room.

My euphoria was gone. I saw a door in the wall.

An iron door, a door made out of iron!

Before testing the latch, I already knew the door would be locked.

And so it was.

And once a door like that is locked, it won't be opened again for any trivial reason.

And I was struck by a number of grim premonitions.

I could have spent some time inspecting the walls, the ceiling, and the floor, but why waste my energy on such a useless activity?

I sat down again. The floor was gently vibrating.

Sure, I'm here, but meanwhile, what will happen to all the others? What will happen to the peasant who mixed up evening and morning? To the woman who sat at home in the evening? The other woman who, perhaps, is still cooking dumplings? The old man in Lasnamäe who still fights vainly for law and order? To Lussi? To Minni?

I had no idea how many days might have passed. And it came to me that the name of Lydia Koidula's husband was also Eduard: he died in 1907 in Kronstadt and was buried beside his wife. When the poetess was reburied in 1946, no one was interested in Eduard, since Michelson was a Germanic Latvian, a medic in the Russian Czarist navy, a gynecologist, who—it was generally believed—was a stranger to Koidula's soul.

> We shall die in transparent Petropolis
> Where Persephone reigns over us.
> We drink with every breath the deathly air
> And every hour is our last.
> —Osip Mandelstam, *Tristia,* 1922

V

Sieh hin, sieh her! Der Mond scheint hell;
Wir und die Toten reiten schnell.
—G. A. Bürger, "Leonore"

MINNI TO LUSSI

August 3, 1986

Hello!

Home for three days now—no Joonatan. Now I regret being so sleepy the night he called. I told him about a silly dream I had about a big white man who smiled at me. It must have annoyed him—it's the sort of thing you shouldn't tell a man. He said he was on his way to hell. Hah! And now he's nowhere. I should have gone to see him, never mind the early bus to Pärnu. Really, we shouldn't have gone at all. We never even managed to get tanned, and, in any case, tans were much more "in" a few years ago than nowadays. Then there was that weird memorial service, and that even weirder person who drove us home and went crazy . . . It was just ghastly, when I think about it. We're lucky we got away with our lives. But where's my Joonatan? We're paying for our pleasure trip now. It's too early for me to act. After all, am I his keeper? He does what he wants—but my heart is heavy: something is wrong. Did you see the moon last night, big, red, and round? And there are more mosquitoes than ever. Do you remember how a few years ago some sneaky mosquito—suddenly started making the rounds—how it sang as it flew by and left these enormous welts? It was supposed to be an avian mosquito that suddenly got a taste for humans. Well, now another species of mosquito has appeared, I don't know its name. It attacks brazenly, but its painful bites leave no marks at all. It's small and fast, and is never satisfied with only one bite. Maybe its appearance is another side-effect of our so-called civilization. It must prefer softer skins than mine. I have no idea who could possibly have a skin softer than mine, but that pest just can't get enough blood out of me. It keeps coming back, again and again. Maybe it has a short proboscis? Anyway, here we are, I gossip but, like I said, my heart is heavy. Logic tells me that nothing bad can have happened to Joonatan, but as I may have already written, my heart is heavy. I reread the above and see that, yes, I did write it. Twice. I'll finish now by saying I hope to hear from you soon.

Minni

LUSSI TO MINNI

August 6, 1986

Hello yourself!

I'd say that Joosep isn't at all the monster you make him out to be. Let's remember that he was drunk out of his mind. Alcohol isn't supposed to be an excuse, but it does excuse a lot. Think what kind of a man he was before he started drinking. An acquaintance explained to me the whole *in vino veritas* idea some time ago, that when drunk, a man becomes the way he really is. And yes, of course, a drunk man will say things he'd keep to himself when sober, but really, by and large, when he's drunk, he's just drunk—meaning he's impaired and shouldn't be taken seriously, and that there's no point in arguing with him either.

I bring this up because I saw him yesterday. He was cold sober. He called me. You of course don't approve of him, so what. He had interesting things to say about the government. Things are extremely complicated, especially in the economic sphere. I didn't understand it all, but I did see that he wasn't at peace with himself, that he wasn't sure how to live his life, since he had once been a supporter of the state but has been rethinking his position lately. That's not easy for any man, Minni. I feel like I understand him; I've often thought of our politicians and wondered how they can do work that has so few rewards! Only a few men have the guts to really change their ways, and Joosep, it seems, is one of these few.

Another thing, what do I tell Juhan? I've never been good at choosing between boys, I mean, giving up this one for that one. I said boys, but at my age I really should say men. Of course it's no sin these days to love more than one at the same time. It used to be strongly condemned and even now our elders equate liberal women with whores. But doesn't every man have some good features? And don't they compensate for each other? I don't mean that a big spender makes up for a miser, necessarily, but Minni, you'll surely admit that a continuously happy man is a bore. And then one that's sad all the time makes you feel dreadful. One is enchanted by everything he sees; the other one doesn't like anything. But taken together they balance each other out. Let's add in a third man who ignores life around him, who lives in the future, always thinking about what he'll do tomorrow, what plans he has to make. And then a fourth man who's not bothered by the future or the past, who's not happy or sad, who simply *is*, you understand?

But I don't want to give up one man, move to another one, and so on. Let's have all of them at once. Naturally, most men would hate that and get furious if they found out. And I do agree that a man who doesn't mind sharing his favorite woman with another man is a little peculiar. He's straining a little too hard to be liberal. Some, no doubt, really are. But the really liberal ones often have no passion. Once in Tõrva I took part in some group sex and I didn't like it. Everyone there just seemed to be doing his duty, so to speak—performing mechanically. Like they were under orders, like slaves—that's how I felt, Minni.

You can see my problem. It's no news to you. On one hand I want to be able to have every man I like, but on the other I don't want them fighting over me—and on the third hand, I don't particularly want to keep a male harem either.

To be honest, this problem doesn't trouble me all that much, since life is filled with many exciting things. Joosep spoke to me in greater detail about that Lydia Koidula woman, the poet of our national awakening. Before our national awakening we were a nation of slaves, he said, that larger countries used to liberate us from each other, expecting us to be grateful for the favor. Actually, the only thing they really cared about was our strategic location at the head of Gulf of Finland, but of course they never explained that to us. Better to live in Lapland, which no one wants except the Lapps, because of the winters. In Lapland we wouldn't have to be liberated so often, and go on being slaves again and again. We're slaves only if you look at us from a distance, since we do still have our own thoughts. But I should get back to Koidula. She lived in Kronstadt near Leningrad. Her husband was a German or a Russian or a Latvian, and Estonians have never had time for him. We've ignored that man, and Joosep explained that Estonians all expected Koidula to be married to *them*. She should never have married a man with foreign blood and without any interest in poetry, who didn't even speak our language. So that's how they lived in Kronstadt. And after Koidula died, the man lived on for years, was eventually buried beside his wife. They rested together some forty years.

I don't believe in life after death, but neither do I want to rot alone God knows where. I do think I'd prefer to be buried with someone, and I realize I'm contradicting myself in saying so, since being buried with more than one man isn't particularly attractive either. I'd like to have a composite of all the men I've loved, so to speak, the essence of them all, with me. That, of course would be considered pretty odd, at least in this country. All that's still ahead of me, of course, and I hope to have a long life that will give me time to think these things over—not that there's anything really worth considering, since I'm just talking nonsense. Joosep said one should fantasize a little once and a while, so I'm fantasizing a little, to you.

Yes, and then came the Soviets, and Koidula was dug up for reburial in Estonia. It wasn't a question of Soviet power, since we could have carried out this prank ourselves, but the Soviets gave us all kinds of material aid, like ships, cranes, a lead coffin, and who knows what else. No one gave a damn about Koidula's husband, though, since the literati believed that Koidula's poetry had never meant anything to him. Other than that, he seemed to have been a decent man. He wasn't reburied, though possibly his bones got mixed up with hers. I don't know what he's doing now. Maybe he's bored. I know it's not nice to speak that way. In this context bored is a silly word. Better to say sad, perhaps even angry. What do you think?

This has been a long letter, but it's wonderful to write about something different for a change. Joosep has gone to a meeting. I share your concern about Joonatan, but honestly: what could possibly happen to him? He's an adult. Maybe he had some business somewhere, something he felt he had to keep to himself. He'll tell you later, if he wants to, but if he doesn't you'd better get used to it, dear friend, if you want to keep him—and I have a feeling that you do. I could be wrong. Let me know.

Your Lussi

P.S. Last night something really odd happened: I met the new mosquito you mention in your letter, but it wasn't alone! Everything was silent. Then there was a sound. It was there and then it wasn't. At first I thought my ears were playing tricks on me or my nose was whistling. I turned over in bed and everything was quiet again. Or not exactly quiet, since I remember a car drove by the house. But then came a whine that stopped when I moved. This happened many times. I sat up and stared at the moon. It was shining the way you described, and my bedroom was bright, but despite blinking my eyes in the light, I didn't see anything out of the ordinary. I was staring so hard that the room began to shimmer in front of me. Nothing. When I finally got back to sleep, I had no idea what was going on. But when I woke up next, I had mosquito bites all over me, since I'd thrown off the blanket while I was sleeping—they were all over me, on my arms, stomach, legs. I turned on the light. Deadly silence, nothing to see. An ordinary mosquito tends to land on the ceiling. Anyway, you can usually catch it before it disappears. The courtyard was dark. I got up. The moon had set behind the neighbor's house. I inspected every corner of my room, shook the drapes and potted plants, but found nothing. Finally I went back to sleep again. In the morning I had no welts anywhere, but my head hurts, and I'm afraid of the dark.

MINNI TO LUSSI

August 9, 1986

Lussi!

Still no news of Joonatan. I think he's deserted me—my punishment for being so cocky and happy-go-lucky.

Life is strange and difficult enough as it is without making more trouble, don't you think, Lussi? Why would anyone travel to Leningrad alone, with things as they are? At least you should have someone you love with you. I know how serious Joonatan can get about these kinds of trips, when he has to go somewhere unexpectedly and do something he can't really anticipate. Naturally, things you haven't done yet can't really be anticipated. But some of us welcome adventure. Do you remember Rudolf? Back in high school? He rode all the way to the other side of the Soviet Union in a cattle car. I can't remember now why those animals were being taken so far away. But they had to be, and the operation needed attendants to feed the animals. That's how Rudolf was able to travel and he did it gladly. Afterwards he told us about his adventures at the railway stations in the Russian interior, also in the old cities of the Khanate in Central Asia cities. It all fascinated him. And do you remember Peter? He loved holidays by the Black Sea, just renting a room and resting. All alone in a strange land! He said it was fun. He sat by the fire and did some thinking. And then there was Tõnu, who still takes a boat out to sea all by himself. Once he went out late in the year when the nights were already getting frosty. He told me how he'd slept under a tree and in the morning found some maple leaves stuck to his beard. Well, all this would seem quite inexplicable to Joonatan. Mind you, he used to like those commercials for Camel boots—"For Men Who Follow Their Own Trails." The ad shows a middle-aged man walking through a jungle; he reaches a bungalow, then swings himself into a hammock. He has no background, no family or homeland. He's not after money or freedom—he probably has plenty of both. Once Joonatan said that that would be a good way to escape everything and ignore the troubles of the world. Yet, would he be vain enough to still admire himself after a few long years of solitude? But now he's gone to Leningrad and I know nothing.

Why did I let him go?

Why didn't I talk him into accepting his ties and responsibilities, giving up fear and indecision and getting married like a civilized person?

You may not know that Joonatan has already been married once, and that the trauma of the divorce made him swear never to do it again. I praised his decision when he told me about it. Let a man think what he wants, after all—that's his right, and how many privileges does a man really have in this life?

But my self-confidence and my devil-may-care attitude, as mentioned in the beginning of this letter (please refer to the previous page), may have resulted in his having too many rights and freedoms. Did I push him into a lonely and dangerous life—instead of giving him a home?

I doubt if all this interests you. But, you should know, I'm perhaps a little less than honest myself when I take such a great interest in your own problems. Still, a few words about

Joosep—I've heard of him somewhere. Joonatan may have mentioned him in connection with something or other. In our own age group we know a surprising number of people, really. I understand that the man was drunk. And so on. And so forth. I mean, don't bother me with your excuses. Choose between men or don't. Keep the ones you like and let the others go. And if you want a particular man, take him and don't be ashamed. How do you choose? You might follow your childhood ideals—always go for tall, dark, slender. Or else you could choose at random, hold a lottery. You win some, you lose some—what else is there, dear Lussi?

Yesterday a child, not yet a year old, living on the third floor, went missing from our house. His mother had laid him on the bed, gone to the kitchen to boil water, and the child was gone when she came back. The window had been open and that's how it was now. On the third floor, understand? The only way in would be the porch. How? There were no footprints anywhere. The militia is investigating. What makes it really weird is the baby's mother saying—apparently she's lost her mind—that she never had a child to begin with. She said that while crying. I've seen her baby myself, beginning with his arrival in a taxi, wrapped in his mother's arms. Then he was and now he is not. Forget about the mother doing away with her baby. The apartment, the house, and the surrounding area have all been thoroughly searched. Nothing. A baby makes noise, and if the mother killed him, the corpse would have been found by now. It's a great mystery.

Be brave,
Minni

LUSSI TO MINNI

August 12, 1986

Hello Minni!

I feel rotten. Lack of sleep? It's the mosquitoes, or something, I have no idea. The wind blew hard all night and all its gusting and the clatter it made on the tin roof kept me up. You never really know how much sleep you get, but I feel like I haven't slept at all. After Joosep left around one o'clock, I tried to go straight to bed but now I'm wide awake, my stomach's churning and my head hurts. Also, my neck is stiff and I'm having trouble turning my head. No doubt you blame Joosep, whom you don't like. I know what you're thinking, but he isn't guilty of anything. He's just a human being, and badly misunderstood. He's followed a road that has nothing to do with the petty day-to-day rivalries and the self-interest of the other politicians. He says he's an adventurer. Who am I to say? It may not interest you anyway. But, to go on with my story, I've made myself some coffee, and came back to write this letter, but I'm still feeling terrible. Maybe I'm getting a cold. All sorts of viruses get passed around in hot weather. I don't have a fever. But the mosquitoes came again in the night and attacked my neck. There are two big punctures on my throat. It's a good thing I don't have to go out today. I'd better get some mosquito repellant. I doubt if Joosep will come back today. He's awfully busy. Our government is currently making preparations to institute some major new initiatives and that means many lives will be disrupted. We'll just have to put up with it. I can't stay awake. Sleep well.

August 13, 1986.

Despite a restless night I'm feeling better. Do you want to hear about it? Joosep is away again at some secret meeting and doesn't have time to listen to my problems. Minni, will you stand in for him? Early in the evening we had some rain but later the sky cleared up. I went to bed early with Teiter's novel *Men*, which is about the lives of men who have decided to contribute to our population growth and to that end start relationships with a bunch of more or less liberal women. It's all for the good of the nation, they say. It has many comical scenes and once I laughed out loud. After one o'clock I got drowsy. I put the book down and turned off the light. Cool damp air blew in from my open window. I was hoping the mosquitoes would leave me alone. They did, but something else happened instead: thick fog began streaming through the window. There's a sulfuric acid plant near my house and I worried the fog might be poisonous. I went to close the window. The courtyard was covered with heavy mist. I couldn't even see the house across the way. The visibility must have been less than two meters, but I didn't smell any sulfur. All of a sudden I knew there was something unusual and exciting hidden in that fog—I just couldn't close the window. You know, Minni, I felt as though I would lose something important if I closed the window, and that I'd regret it all my life if I didn't let whatever it was inside. There was a sense of urgency about it. Like I was doing something bad, something violent, to satisfy my baser instincts. Have you ever felt like that? Have you ever wanted to pour gas on the floor and then strike a match? Have you ever wanted to cut the ropes holding a painter's gurney ten or twenty floors up? How exciting that would be! So there I stood, the window open and mist streaming in. It touched my stomach, crept lower, and then formed an ever-expanding ring around me. Some gases are denser than air, aren't they? Should I lie down on the floor, I wondered? Why not? I'm not sure if I did or not. In any case, in the morning I was back in my bed. No fog. Nothing unusual. But I'm feeling much better than I did yesterday morning.

I'm sorry to talk so much about myself. I wish your Joonatan would soon come home.

Lussi

MINNI TO LUSSI

Lussi!

Joonatan is alive but in a hospital. A doctor found my number in Joonatan's pocket and called me. Would you believe he was lying face down on Stroom Beach? At first the people who found him thought they had a corpse, a drowned person on their hands. But his clothes were dry and he was a few meters inland from the water. When he showed some signs of life, they assumed he was just a drunk. The militia was called in. But Joonatan was cold sober, although his talk was slurred, and he was much too weak to help himself. An ambulance took him to a psychiatric hospital.

Poor Joonatan!

I visited him last evening and had a short talk with his doctor. He told me to take it easy on him: Joonatan experienced some serious trauma and needs time to recover. The doctor said he'd had similar cases in the past, and that they all had turned out well.

Joonatan recognized me but he was extremely apathetic. He seemed to understand his situation. Smiling sadly he said something like, "Minni, I'm sick. The sickness is such that I don't want to remember what happened to me. I seem to recollect many unpleasant things. If I remembered them fully, these memories would force me to act, run, save myself, fight for my life—but somehow I don't want to. I prefer forgetting. I realize I can't stay this way forever, but that's why right now I won't do anything at all. Leave me alone. Let me rest. Wait a while, Minni. Bear with me."

He stroked my hand.

"Right now please leave. Your presence here forces me to remember. I'd like to tell you everything. But if I did, I'd have to give up my peaceful state of mind. I would have to get up and think. Except I don't want to think right now. Please be kind and go away. Please."

He was silent for a while, then said, "Minni, I'd like to pretend that I don't recognize you. It would comfort me, although . . ." He looked around and started whispering, "Really, I recognize you very well. I'm not going to pretend with you. I just need some peace."

A nurse came in, gave him some pills and water, and left quietly.

"Minni, when I get well and the danger is over, let's get married. For now, just go."

So I left.

Lussi, can you appreciate how upset I was? On one hand I was worried about Joonatan's condition—never mind the positive prognosis—and on the other hand I'd just been proposed to, something I wasn't expecting and had never dared hope for. I've always known he was against any long-term commitment. I came right home and am still completely confused and conflicted while writing this.

At first I thought he'd had too much to drink and wasn't really paying attention to what was coming out of his mouth, but his eyes told me that whatever he's been through lately would be just unimaginable for you and me, Lussi.

I do believe that he'll tell me everything one day, and that then I'll hear as much as the Fates will allow.

Till then I wish you much forbearance and peace.

Live well!

Minni

VI

The power of the Vampire comes
From no one believing in him.
—Bram Stoker, *Dracula*

JOOSEP'S DIARY

Greifer sent for me. This matter, he said, is extremely confidential, so keep your mouth shut. I'll comply of course but a diary is insurance against forgetting vital details.

Greifer: Warnings have appeared on many levels.

Who?—Let's say X.

When?—Apparently in late July.

The scale?—Undetermined.

We should be prepared for minimum effect but also maximum.

In situations of great tension, let's say—during situations of significant tension, we should be prepared for the maximum. The problem is—we have no criteria. When should we expect the maximum? When the minimum?

And how much?

Attachment No.1, Complete. Regarding the reopening of Lydia Koidula's grave in Kronstadt: On Aug. 8, 1946, between 18:30 and 23:00, a medical commission consisting of the following individuals carried out of the disinterment of Lydia Koidula and the examination of the contents of her grave: Dr. P. Pedusaar, foreman, a Judicial Court medical examiner from Tallinn; Drs. H. Pross and N. Goromulinski, surgeons, epidemiologists from Tallinn; and the representative of the Kronstadt Department of Health, Dr. M. Misujev. It was recorded that her coffin was buried at a depth of 1.6 meters. The bottom and side planks of the coffin were severely decayed, and the lid had collapsed. Upon removal of the remaining coverings, Lydia Koidula's bones were found to be loose, except for a few small ones that still adhered to one another. The excavated skeleton was put in a hermetically sealed and lead-lined oak coffin we had brought with us.

Aug. 8., Anno 1946, Kronstadt.
Signed: Foreman P. Pedusaar
Witnessed: Dr. M. Misujev

Attachment No. 2: Excerpt from the written reminiscence of Juhan Schmuul: The soil is hard and digging goes slowly. Help from the Estonian soldiers of Comrade Smirnov's troop is appreciated. Digging continues in the dark, with flashlights.

After a medical examination, Koidula's remains are placed

in the new coffin. In honor of our great poet, the Kronstadt TRSN Executive Committee workers bring flowers to lay in her lap.

At her feet we place an oak branch and some additional flowers. The coffin is closed and the Estonian soldiers carry her to a truck. We drive through nocturnal Kronstadt.

Attachment No.3: Excerpt from the written reminiscences of Mart Raud: . . . Koidula's grave has been dug up, all the way down to the decayed boards of her coffin. The autumn evening is turning into night and there's no more sunlight. Batteries supply light to work by. One by one we pick up the bones while up on the rim of the grave Comrade Smirnov, envoy of the Russian Navy, Comrade Kadasadze, and a slew of Kronstadters—true aficionados of poetry—read Koidula in faultless Russian. Translations of her poems have recently been issued in Moscow, I understand. The readers appear to be affected by the solemn occasion. They know the fate of the Estonian people and have a general idea of our struggles. The reading covers every poem in the book, as well as the preface about Koidula's life and work

And when, by midnight, we have transferred her remains to a new, oak coffin, our Kronstadt comrades arrive with beautiful flowers. We transfer Koidula to the ship. By now it's night. Ready to weigh anchor, we are asked to delay our departure till the morning. This city that was so dismal and strange to Koidula wants to bid farewell to her in daylight. And that's how it happened.

Aug. 3

As we could have guessed, it's begun. At her wedding, a bride named P was kidnapped.

<u>Attachment: Transcript from tape of bride's interrogation:</u>

Examiner: Let's go back to the beginning one more time. You were singing in the cellar. What did the cellar look like?

Bride: The house was only built six months ago, so the cellar walls are bare cement, no plaster. No furniture either. For the wedding guests, my father-in-law had put up a long board on a couple of sawhorses. A few people were sitting quietly, but most were singing.

E: What kind of song were they singing?

B: It had no words. [She hums.] It went something like that.

E: And do you always sway back and forth when you sing?

B: Yes.

E: Where was the groom?

E: He'd gone upstairs for beer.

E: No beer in the cellar?

B: No. The keg was in the kitchen.

E: Was X in the kitchen all that time?

B: No, X wasn't there at all, I have no idea where he was. Only N, B, A, V, S, and N were in the cellar, along with a couple of small boys who were just hanging around. We kept on singing, I don't know why. The rest of the crowd was upstairs at the dining room table. The party got going at two o'clock. Plenty to drink, so people started to swap places and talk loud, and no one suspected anything unusual was going on.

E: And the groom was pouring beer upstairs?

B: Yes. In any case, I was feeling hot—the cellar had an oil-stove in it. I snuck upstairs quietly and no one took any notice of me. I opened the front door. The light was dim and it was drizzling.

E: Then what happened?

B: A noisy car drove up, a gray Volga. Two guys got out and took me by my arms, not rudely but politely, one of them saying—no, it wasn't X, I'd never seen him before—this is a "bride abduction," so please just be quiet, and of course I didn't dare to yell because I've heard of that custom, and I thought, well, I shouldn't scream and carry on since I'll just seem young and naïve, I'd better behave like a mature woman who knows what's what, who's above making a fool of herself, and so I kept quiet, but later I could see that I should never have given in like that.

E: Was X in the car?

B: Yes, he was.

E: Had you seen him before?

B: I think so.

E: What do you mean—"think so"?

B: I thought he might have been a friend of my husband's. I felt like I'd seen him somewhere before.

E: Had you spoken to him then, whenever you'd first met him?

B: [Shakes her head.]

E: Where did they take you?

B: Out of town. I mean, our house is already at the edge of town, near Pariku Forest. Actually, it's only a grove by the railway station, surrounded by fields—not much of a forest.

E: And what time was that?

B: It was getting dark, but the day was cloudy, so I can't be sure. X didn't say anything during the drive. I tried to talk, be casual, treat it like a joke, but it was somewhat awkward driving who knows where with a bunch of strangers, regardless of whether or not it's an old wedding custom.

E: Hundreds of years ago bride abduction was widespread.

B: Right, and that's why I didn't feel like whining. We reached Pariku Forest and left the main road. "Listen," I said. "That's enough, let's go back."

E: And what did he do?

B: That's when it happened.

E: Please elaborate.

B: I'd rather not.

E: Unfortunately, I need to know everything that happened.

B: I understand.

E: So let's have it.

B: Well, he took my hand and stroked my fingers one by one, saying that my fingers were transparent, meaning that he could see the bones when looking at them against the light, and he lifted my hand up to the window, but like I've already told you the light was poor so I didn't see any bones or anything, although I guess they must have been there. For a first conversation with someone, it was a bit weird. I'm a daring kind of girl and I understand that bride abduction is supposed to be all in fun, but it's supposed to be nothing more than a harmless prank, especially for a friend of the husband. "I don't see any bones," I said nonchalantly. "It's dark." X nodded and asked the other man for a light. He struck . . ."

E: A match?

B: Yes. A match. I put my hand in front of the match and I thought I could see my wrist bones and the bones in my fingers. I don't know why it was so important to him. By now it was raining pretty hard. I heard the patter on the roof of the car. Well, then X took out a razor.

E: Describe the razor.

B: An old-fashioned straight razor in a leather pouch with a white handle.

E: Did he say anything?

B: He muttered something.

E: In what language?

B: I didn't recognize it. And then I realized I'd never seen this man before. Maybe the dim light had been playing tricks on me. He had pale blue eyes of a Siamese cat. And he kept on muttering, very politely, like he was declaring his love or begging forgiveness for something. He held my hand like he was going to kiss it, and then he lowered his head and spoke to my hand, which was still in his grip. And in his other hand there was that open razor. At that moment I knew what was in store for me. Should I have fought back? Should I have screamed? Would that have helped? No. I was alone in a forest with two murderers. Nothing could have helped me. But suddenly—no one's ever going to believe any of this—one of the strangers backed off. The car door opened and I was pushed out. I fell into the tall wet grass and before I could get up their car took off with a howl. When I sat up I could see the lights of another car approaching. It was my husband-to-be and his real friends. Yes, I was saved. The criminals had vanished into the night. Their tracks disappeared on the main road. We drove back to the wedding. On the way we agreed to keep my little adventure to ourselves—after all, our guests weren't guilty of anything. I'm not sure how my pretended cheerfulness came off—our wedding guests can evaluate my performance better than I can. My husband said he didn't know X at all, but isn't it common to have a stranger or two at a wedding? Someone's cousin, a guest's new girlfriend maybe, someone we hadn't met yet? But what had tipped my husband off? Why had he felt uneasy and gone to check on me? He said that an inner voice had told him to find me. Your wife is in trouble, it said. So he came. That's how I survived. That's all I have to say.

E: Do you remember any of the foreign words X said to you?

B: *Härimai,* he said *härimai* a bunch of times.

E: *Härimai?*

B: That's what it sounded like.

E: What could that mean?

B: How should I know? It wasn't said casually. It came from the heart.

E: Did it sound like he was saying no to something, forbidding something?

B: More like permitting something.

E: And he had the eyes of a Siamese cat?

B: Yes. My friend has a Siamese. Can't stand cold weather, so she knitted a vest for her. So she wouldn't get bronchitis. The cat had eyes just like his.

E: Thank you. If we need more information, we'll call you.

B: I hope I was of some help.

E: Absolutely. Every bit helps.

What bothers me the most is that none of this looks like Michelson's work.

What's my own role in this business? I need a couple of days to think it over, analyze the information.

Härima?—Maori. To be precise: *he haere mai* (Hello). For that I thank Mihkel Mutt.

Aug. 4

I found a telephone number on a piece of paper in my pocket, so I called it. Someone named Lucy answered. Pleasant voice. Can't remember if we've met before, or where. But if we have, great. Friendship with such a pleasant voice should always be renewed. Fixed a date for the next day. Things are progressing. X has been captured. His real name is Poder. Naturally he's not Michelson. I guessed that immediately. Poder claims he was in Leningrad selling cucumbers. Many farmers go to the Leningrad market. More demand. Higher prices. That's how it is in a big city. The customer base of Tallinn can't absorb everything that's grown here. Merchandise rots unsold. That's where Leningrad comes in. Poder claims no one put him up to it. He admits to threatening the bride and will take the rap.

But I don't think Poder acted alone.

He's prepared to atone for his crime in the eyes of society.

Link between Poder and Michelson? Certainly possible.

Yesterday a baby, left asleep in a park, disappeared.

Poder's name doesn't appear on the Tallinn donors list.

His acquaintances? Unremarkable.

AIDS test—negative.

What is Poder hiding?

This is the only important thing. Otherwise Poder is of no interest to us.

I suggested to Greifer we contact some astrologers and psychics.

He said no right away. I can see his point—the Soviet Union has managed without necromancers thus far, so approaching them now would be like admitting defeat. Let them all go to hell. I don't trust them anyway. The investigation shouldn't be broadened. We have to be careful. We can't afford to have any leaks.

Lucy will be waiting for me tomorrow, assuming she wants to.

What does she look like?

Nice, I hope.

Maybe even very nice?

Aug. 5

Lussi (that's the way she spells her name) exceeded all my expectations.

Attachment: Transcript from tape of meeting with Lussi.

Lussi: I had a lovely time. You go to that bar often?

Me: Once a month or so.

L: Same here.

M: Could it be we met there, sometime?

L: Maybe we did.

M: There?

L: Or some other place.

M: I have a strong feeling we've met before.

L: Your feeling might be right.

[A pause.]

M: Where could it have been?

L: Think. Think.

M: Visiting someone?

L: Warm.

M: At Malka's?

L: Cold.

M: I give up.

L: Do you want me to tell you?

M: Please do.

L: Minni's place.

[A pause.]

M: I considered that.

[A pause.]

M: Let's have another drink.

L: Why not?

[A pause.]

M: Wait a minute, which Minni?

L: The same.

[A pause.]

(I knew who I was talking with now. I met her the night I left Pärnu. Can't remember much. I went somewhere, got completely drunk, went home.)

M: Blue or red?

L: My God!

M: Are you scared?

L: Not at all.

M: Then choose.

L: Wait. Let me think.

M: Think fast.

L: Red.

M: OK.

L: Wait. Let's go with blue.

M: One blue, one red?

L: No. I don't like that.

M: Think. Red underneath, blue on top.

L: Should be the same color.

M: Should we draw lots?

L: No, I'll choose. Just give me a second.

M: I can't.

L: Red. A tanned body on a warm red background . . .

M: That's what you wanted in the first place.

L: Let me try.

M: Please do.

[A pause.]

L: Well?

M: Well what? I like it.

L: What do you like, exactly?

M: This. That. And those.

L: It tickles.

M: But this?

L: What's this?

M: Do you like it?

L: It feels nice. Almost.

M: Almost?

L: I'd say yes.

Here the tape becomes difficult to interpret. Listening to it might be exciting, but on paper it loses something. For example:

L: Hu-huu.

M: Bu-buu.

L: Gu-guu.

Another section of another tape is more deserving of close examination:

L: Minni was next to me.

M: No, I was.

L: On the sofa? Definitely Minni.

M: Actually, I don't remember much. Both of you were close to me. Were there two of you?

L: No. The other one was Minni.

M: Where is she now? Why isn't she here, on these red sheets, beautiful and fragrant? Like a sunrise, like new-mown grass . . . like a wood sorrel . . . like the balloons of a little girl watching the May Day parade?

L: Minni has her Joonatan.

M: Where is this Joonatan? Bring him here. I'll talk to him.

L: Joonatan has disappeared in Leningrad.

M: Disappeared how?

L: Don't know. He went to Leningrad and that was it.

M: Enough about him.

L: I agree.

M: I don't much want to hear about this Minni either, to be perfectly frank. All the more so since she doesn't even exist. And neither does her Joonatan. But wait a second—what's his family name?

L: Hark.

M: The writer?

L: Yes. Yes, yes. I need a drink. Bring me some water.

Spending the afternoon in a public library.

Joonatan Hark. His books.

I take notes. His novel *Koidula in Võru*. Plot: Koidula (reincarnated in our century) revisits the house, now a museum, of her old mentor Kreutzwald—her platonic love. The summer is hot and humid. Apparently set before the most recent Soviet reforms. The streets deserted, people are either in the country or vacationing. A cat sleeps next to a warehouse wall. Some tourists from Moscow shop for furniture covers. Potato stalks in gardens are beginning to wilt. Koidula recalls how she spent some time in this town in 1868 (during her lifetime?). Mrs. Kreutzwald received her grudgingly. Jealous. (Kreutzwald was 65, Koidula 25.) (Goethe was 72 and Ulrike von Lewetzow 17, in Marienbad.) Apparently Koidula left Võru disappointed. Now Joonatan Hark's outlandish story brings her back. Joonatan Hark isn't a full-fledged fantasy writer, nor is he a surrealist. His goal seems to be to describe a provincial town in summer with its sweet but abject sadness. Rather than a reincarnated Koidula visiting, it could as easily have been himself. For himself he's substituted a well-known poet. If you aren't native to Võru, and don't live there either, if you visit during the summer months, you're basically a pariah in that town. It seems to me that in strange towns you're always alone. Great adventurers and travelers enjoy novel experiences. They take notes. Extroverts always blend in with the ambience. They don't think of themselves. It's different with introverts. Clearly Joonatan Hark is an introvert. Võru doesn't matter. He's only preoccupied with himself. His own melancholy is paramount. *I* suffered in Võru! But does he admit it? Admitting weakness seems feminine to him and makes him feel ashamed. So he takes a woman's name. I, Lydia, suffered in Võru! He could have said: I, Mary, suffered in Võru!, but no. He calls himself Koidula. Hiding behind history.

So, in the eighties, in late summer, Koidula walked the streets of Võru, thinking (here's an excerpt):

"This summer I'm in Võru, I wander under the sun that's overhead, shoes covered with dust, nobody knows me and I don't know anybody; this is another one of the towns I visit endlessly, it could be Tartu, Pärnu, Kronstadt, Helsinki, Vändra, Leppälahti, or any of the towns I've been to, Freiburg or Vienna or Breslau or Frankfurt am Main where my dead son once ran around and visited the birthplace of Goethe. Always alone and invisible—mirrors don't reflect me. No one sees me, no one loves me, my sentence is to wander this earth forever, and I call out to myself: Come, see me at last, how long must I be invisible, how much longer will my blood be clear like water, it used to be red, I well remember how one day, when slicing meat, I cut my finger and my blood blended with the drippings from the roast beef. Edushing bellowed *Liebe!* and bandaged my finger. Now it's noon in Võru, it's August and my blood is no longer red, and even if it suddenly turned red again, no one would notice, and no one would tell me, yes, no one. In the dust by the wall of the warehouse a cat is stretching out, no flies are buzzing, they're hiding in the shade somewhere. I didn't come into this world on a bus, and I won't leave it on an airplane—Kreutzwald is dead like me, it doesn't matter how many times I come here, he doesn't deign to leave his grave, I must live alone, if it can be called a life, and when on Kreutzwald Street I call, voicelessly, come, come at last, even the trees don't answer me. The air is still. Not a breath."

Joonatan Hark and the recent phenomena—are they linked?

Naturally the situation predates J. H., who only reflects it. The idea of a reincarnation of Koidula has already been exploited by Teet Kallas, Raimond Kaugver, Priidu Beier, and Mati Unt.

The Koidula fad: Lindepuu, Undla-Põldmae, the plays of Unt. And of Wuolioe!

Irrelevant to the current case.

At least for this moment.

Yet, the appearance of these personalities must not be ignored.

Background for the above.

Predictions?

Aug. 7

Interview with Greifer.

Still extremely confidential.

By the way, Greifer accompanied me into the hall. When I got into the elevator, he waved to me. With me in the elevator were a woman and man. We went down but didn't stop at the first floor, as we should have, but dropped all the way to the basement, the end of the line. The door didn't open. At first it was funny, then it started to worry us. We banged on the walls and yelled. We could hear a commotion begin above us. Our distress was noted but no one seemed to be doing anything.

The woman was in her forties. She didn't know the man. I did nothing. If I'd had to urinate, it would have been extremely embarrassing.

After ten minutes we were let out.

I called Greifer and told him what happened. He laughed.

Who is Michelson's coconspirator?

And potential allies.

Aug. 9

[. . .] 2 years old. Missing on a clear day. Third floor.

[. . .] 9 months old, also third floor.

In both cases the mothers had put the children on a bed, one to sit, the other to lie down. Both mothers had gone to their kitchens, one to boil soup, the other one to boil water.

In both cases the windows were ajar, though one was closed and locked, the other window open and loose.

Both babies vanished without a trace.

The second mother, in a state of shock, now claims she's
never had a child.

I called Lussi.

Aug. 12

Estonians, despite an extended isolation from the rest of
the world, are a potentially vital society. They have kept their
genetic memories and inner lives.

Meanwhile no more babies have disappeared.

A few more observations:

1) Plenty of mosquitoes out.

2) I often wake with a headache.

3) Last night the full moon was reported to have
changed its orbit, appearing to soar toward the zenith, then
continue on its regular path, instead of simply moving west.
This was reported by numerous sleepless individuals.

4) The streets are peaceful, so far.

Aug. 13

The German text on Koidula's headstone (*"Unser Leben,
wenn es köstlich gewesen ist, so ist es Mühe und Arbeit gewesen"*) is
supposed to be from the Psalms, number 90. Seventy is the
sum of our years, or eighty if we are strong, and at best they
are pain and misery for they pass quickly and we depart as if
in flight.

Last evening I drank vodka. Memory gap.

Aug. 14

The latest rumor around town:

In Õismäe, M. M., a single woman in her forties, came home in the evening to find her Doberman on the floor gasping for air. She phoned Dr. Hints, whom she knew well. The vet told her to bring the animal in right away. She did.

Despite a thorough examination, Dr. Hints couldn't figure out what was wrong. He planned to perform a tracheotomy, preferably without the owner present. He advised her to go home and wait for his call. The woman, who lived alone, obeyed.

No sooner had she opened the door to her apartment, however, the phone rang—to her amazement, it was Dr. Hints. The woman expected to hear news about her dog, but Dr. Hints told her to get out of her apartment immediately—back to the clinic if she had no other place to go. The woman took him seriously and got out.

What had happened?

During the operation, Dr. Hints had found three human fingers stuck in the dog's throat. He has assumed these came from an intruder who could still be in the house, so having warned his client, he called the militia, who found a bleeding man with three fingers missing on the floor of the back room.

Must check.

Aug. 15
   Citing Koidula:
   Behold—the dawn of life has come—
   And suddenly an angel
   On the edge of my grave

Bids me to rise.
The stone of death rolls away,
The dawn sparkles, smiles—
Young freedom dressed in white
All the world welcomes you.

I love you in my grave.

If I die, I love you still.

The Õismäe story is a crock.

Moreover: cultural anthropologists have discovered the origin of the rumor.

(Jan Harold Brunvandt, *The Choking Doberman*, New York, 1984)

Had a few drinks with Greifer. Memory not affected.

What is Michelson after?

What are we guilty of?

Is it a national problem? Isn't life supposed to be difficult?

Aug. 16

A disturbing thought: Can Greifer be trusted? Who is behind Michelson?

[This last entry is in code.]

Could I possibly find a common language with Michelson? Only if necessary?

Something terrible has happened to Lussi!!

VII

Baptized in Lucy's blood, Arthur
Seward and Quincy in effect lose
Virginity.
—G. A. Waller, *The Living and the Undead*

1

"What now?"

Greifer, a taciturn man, posed this vital question. Sitting in the corner, almost invisible, his torso and knees were lit by the table-lamp, but his placid yet watchful face was in the shadows.

"Now comes garlic." Joosep's quiet voice precluded any arguments.

At this, the young woman in the room, whose name—to our surprise—was Alli, snorted.

Joosep gave a sad smile.

"Let's not turn our noses up at any possible solutions, not even the traditional means. Greifer's scanned the room for bugs, but that hardly makes us safe. Something is missing.

This is a well-constructed house in an upper-class neighborhood, with its drapes drawn and guards posted at both ends of the street, as well as in the back of the garden. A modern, civilized person would construe from all this that we should be perfectly safe. In fact, we're not. That's why we resort to garlic."

He took a brown bag out of his briefcase.

"Garlic, dear friends, is the universal vampire remedy. True enough, it can awaken undesired passions, though on the other hand, the Ancient Greeks gave their wives garlic to chew on before they went out on the town. The rank odor helped their women stay true to their husbands. The protective character of garlic is broad, so we'll make use of it."

He scattered garlic cloves around the room, on the windowsill, the doorstep, and even on the table in front of us.

I spoke: "This is all very nice, but let's talk about Lussi now."

Joosep's expression didn't change as he casually replied, "We'll get to things in their proper order, Joonatan, in their proper order. Let's start with you."

They all looked at me: Alli, Minni, Joosep, and probably Greifer too, in the shadows.

After a few seconds I said with perfect sincerity, "I have many theories, but few facts."

"At least tell us about that locked room where you woke up."

"I know I came to for a few minutes, but after that everything gets hazy again. The walls of the cell were shiny—some sort of plastic, I guess. The door was iron. And the latch was unusual, it reminded me of a . . . ship's steering wheel."

"Furniture?"

"No furniture. The room was absolutely empty."

Minni spoke up: "You did mention a vibrating floor."

Yes, it did vibrate, but the certainty I'd had at the time was gone. When I put my palms on the floor, the metal—yes, the floor was also metal—seemed to vibrate. I didn't put my ear to the floor. It could have been some sort of an engine. I described my memories briefly, omitting all speculation.

Greifer sighed but didn't say anything.

He understood what I had omitted.

So did everyone else.

"And you woke up on the beach at Stroom?"

Yes, that's how it was, and my clothes were dry, and my brain was empty. Sucked dry. I had been made use of while I was asleep. I had been someone's unpublished "Estonian Encyclopedia."

As if by common consent, we stopped for a moment to listen to the wind wailing through the old apple orchard behind the house. Despite the strangeness of the occasion, I felt chagrined to be under such scrutiny. Why had I been so helpless against something so vile, only now to be subjected to this interrogation? When you're beautiful and strong it can be nice to get attention. But when you're helpless, when you only evoke pity and fear?

Birds migrate, people look up at the sky, and karst rivers flow through secret limestone caverns that only a few scientists have ever explored—so why out of so many people was I condemned to wander so deep under the knotted surface of the psyche?

Compared to Lussi, though, my worries didn't amount to much, and that's where the talk was veering now.

Minni, for the occasion, had worn a dark blue velvet costume and a white collar that made her look like a Czarist high-school student. And only I knew what she looked like in a different costume, yes, and even without any costume at all—that Minni was now telling her side of the story.

"When Joonatan was found, I wrote to Lussi, I believe it was on August 16. She didn't reply. In her previous letters she'd been describing her dreams and some unusual phenomena. Here are the aggressive mosquitoes and the poisonous fog."

Minni took a bunch of letters from her handbag and put them on the table. We already knew their contents, so Minni clicked her handbag shut and continued.

"I can't say I thought of Lussi a lot. I had worries of my own."

She glanced at me from the corner of her eye and smiled slightly. I knew how much trouble she had taken over me. I was in the hospital for four days, and I'm not a very good patient. But now we were going to hear something new. Minni took out a cigarette—she hardly ever smoked—and looked around for a match. Joosep reacted the fastest. I noticed that the hand that held her cigarette trembled.

"Joonatan was still in the hospital, and I was in my bed reading. It was almost eleven. The doorbell rang, and I felt I shouldn't answer it—I don't know why. I tiptoed to the foyer and looked through the peephole to the hallway. The light on the stairwell was out as usual and the only illumination came from the floor above. All I could see was a shape. Put yourself in my place. What would you have done? I couldn't see a face, couldn't tell if it was a man or a woman. Yet, I knew it had to be Lussi. I also knew I absolutely shouldn't let her in. Please understand: if I'd seen for certain that it was she, I probably would have opened the door regardless. But not knowing gave me the courage to act the way I did. I don't know you, I told the figure silently. I have the right to not admit you. And I prefer you didn't identify yourself, because then I have an alibi. I stood in my dark foyer and she/he stood unmoving in the stairwell. I'm not sure how long it took, probably not very long—time moves very slowly in this kind of situation, except it moves much faster than usual—anyway, I doubt if it took more than twenty seconds. Then the visitor left, and slowly went down the stairs. I tried to spot her on the street out of my window but it was raining hard and I didn't see anyone leave the building. No longer in the mood to read, I was just sad and thought over what had happened. Had it been Lussi? And if it was, why didn't I let her in? And, anyway, if it really was her, why didn't she say anything? She hesitated and so did I. As if we were afraid of each other. But that had never been the case before. And then I noticed a tiny silver cross in my fist—one I sometimes wear, though not very often, as you may have noticed."

I certainly have, I thought jealously. Had Greifer or Joosep seen that cross?

"I usually keep the cross in a tray on my side table. I must have picked it up automatically as I passed by and I must have had it with me all the time I was by the door."

Minni put out her cigarette, nervously dousing it in the ash-tray.

Somewhere a dog began to bark.

We listened to the dog, since it seemed to be a lonely dog, not at all dangerous.

Minni continued: "In the morning, on my way to the hospital to see Joonatan, I found grains of wheat strewn outside my door. Handfuls of them."

Joosep, cradling his head between his hands moaned: "Poor Lussi, poor Lussi . . ."

Minni nodded.

And got to her feet. She circled the room, touched a porcelain figure as if checking it for dust, then lowered her self into an easy chair at the far side of the room.

"Yes, I realized she meant me no harm, finally," she said from the deeps of the chair. "She overcame her own needs, somehow. My poor friend."

The dog had fallen silent, leaving only the rustle of the trees.

Something had to be done. A decision was called for.

As if responding to my thoughts, Greifer spoke: "Too bad all that is irrelevant."

Alli snapped, "Really?"—as if anticipating the direction the conversation would take.

"Yes. The choice we must make is brutal but inevitable."

"Why?" Alli asked.

"Lussi will never be human again."

"So what?"

"What, so *what*?"

"Does everyone have to be human?"

"What else should they be?"

"Whatever they want to be."

"And then?"

"The rejected also have the right to live."

By now Greifer's sleepy eyes were wide open.

"Surely you know she's dangerous."

"Dangerous to whom?"

"To humans."

"So what?"

"I don't understand."

"You don't understand because you are a party functionary, an apparatchik, and you earn your pay by favoring humans over other organisms . . . whatever they may be."

"And you, my dear lady, are a hater of humanity. I do respect your point of view, and I'm not the only one. Your protection of the Lasnamäe meteorite site made a lot of us take notice. Even Radio Free Europe broadcast your little performance. You must be proud of delaying the construction of a badly needed road for a few days. And now you'd like to protect vampires . . ."

There was a quiet knock on the door.

I noticed Joosep's thin, almost transparent fingers crawl as if accidentally to the garlic cloves on the table.

It was our hostess with coffee.

When she'd gone, Joosep spoke up.

"You all can argue as much as you like, but the practical side of the matter is my responsibility. Unfortunately."

We stared at Joosep. Not just I, but all of us, I believe, knew then what he meant to do.

He, most likely, had already made his plans.

He gazed at his own pale, wasted hands under the table lamp with deep suspicion.

Here are some abbreviated minutes from the rest of our meeting:

Alli wouldn't budge. She was an advocate of deviants and minorities. In my heart, naturally, I supported her, the way a writer must. At the same time I told myself that the radical viewpoint of our warlike maiden was somewhat pretentious and unoriginal. Through she spoke the spirit of the times, and it spoke a little too loud. Her outburst made me take a look at myself. In my youth I believed in the reality principle. Of course, when Greifer spoke of an economically independent Estonia with its inherent problems and dangers, when he pointed out that everything is connected and that what had happened to Lussi was just an example of a much larger system, when he stressed our national and societal position, I couldn't take him seriously either. Lussi a victim! A victim of independence! Victimized by the latest policy shift? Then why did it have to be Lussi? We had no idea how many people Michelson had already infected. But that word "Estonia" had an effect on me. Identity is extremely important to a small nation. Secretly I found myself agreeing with Greifer: maybe Michelson isn't a *bad person*, per se, not to mention our beautiful Lussi. In the spider web of cause and effect they were merely playing out their dismal and thankless roles.

Joosep too was firm. "Don't try to change my mind. Leave me be. This is my business. End of story."

Minni had been the last one to see Lussi (assuming it was her), if only as a silhouette in semidarkness. Did Joosep know where to find her? Around midnight Greifer told his driver to fetch the car. We went out to the street. Yellow maple leaves descended through the bright circles of the streetlights. Misty rain sprinkled. Autumn was here. Joosep whistled three times. The guards came out from their posts. They had seen nothing unusual. The evening had been peaceful. They piled in and with a rustle the limousine vanished around the corner.

Greifer's final words—"In any case, we'll win"—were aphoristic, and left me unconvinced.

Minni, shivering with cold, pressed herself against me.

"If only it was over—let it be a dream," she whispered in my ear.

"It is a dream." I tried to sound convincing.

Joosep leaped over a puddle to the garden hedge.

"The things one does in this job," he said in a half-comical manner. He took a jackknife out of his pocket and selected a sapling.

"I'm told it can be aspen or ash," he said, facing us. "There are no oaks here in any case."

I shrugged.

Joosep selected a straight young ash, chopped it down, and sliced off the top, leaving a forty centimeter-long stick. Under a streetlight he sharpened one end. Cold raindrops ran down our bare necks. Feeling depressed, we said our goodbyes to him and departed. The street was deserted. At the second corner we found a taxi.

We got home after one o'clock.

Exhausted, I sat in the easy chair and watched Minni undress. She meticulously folded and hung up her high-school girl's dress before carrying it to the closet. Mysteriously to a mere male, she bundled her undergarments and put them in a drawer. On her stomach Minni had an appendix scar. I recalled the book Joosep had been studying just before our meeting. He'd underlined: *A sharpened stake should be employed with a single blow through the heart (or navel); this procedure is properly known as "transfixion."* Minni had goose bumps all over her. I took her in my arms and we fell onto the bed. The draining and wretched day behind us promoted anything but sexual desire. Yet we felt as if making love was an obligation. I guess it was a kind of protest against that, "In any case, we'll win." Neither of us really caught fire, though. Every embrace felt a little ridiculous and affected. She helped me in, but when I determinedly kept on caressing her at the same time—among other things nipping her earlobes, and very softly kissing her throat—she stiffened. My God, what kind of life is this? We disengaged. I stroked her hair, went over to the window. The rain was over. Nothing moved outside. I went back to bed. And believe it or not, we fell asleep right away.

2

The phone rang early.

Still sleepy, I stumbled over a chair to pick it up.

"Greifer here."

I waited for what would come next.

Outside it was still dark.

"I'm sending a car right away."

He hung up.

By now Minni was awake and had figured out what was going on.

She got dressed, sat in front of her mirror and applied some rouge. I brewed coffee and poured out two cups. By the time Minni managed to take a sip, a horn tooted outside.

"Goddamn it," said Minni.

Since there was nothing else we could do, we put on our overcoats and climbed in.

On the back seat, wearing dark glasses for some unfathomable reason, his bald skull shining in the gloom, sat Greifer.

As we got going, a red dawn peeped over the horizon. Llama-like clouds were running west.

Patiently we waited for Greifer to start talking. The road took us out of town past some workers, who were innocently waiting for the bus, and flocks of children on their way to school.

"Joosep lost," Greifer said.

What was there to say after that?

Soon we were out among green fields, hidden behind a curtain of mist.

Greifer had lapsed into silence again.

A rabbit hopped across the road into a ditch.

Then birds, a flock of them low over the road: fast, black, and frenzied.

Past the woods we came upon an uneven village lane.

The dawn glowed red through the thickening fog.

To be honest, I wasn't sure about Greifer anymore. During the long night, anything could have happened. A strange man in a leather overcoat, with a billiard-ball head and dark glasses. What guarantee was there that he was on our side? I don't know what Minni thought about him.

We pulled off the road.

What would Greifer do now?

After another lengthy pause he said, "Well, what are we waiting for? Let's go."

It wasn't the time to start an argument.

We left the car by a swamp. A dilapidated barn loomed in the fog. The tall grass soaked our pants and shoes. Greifer in the lead heedlessly pushed aside alder saplings. The driver was left dozing in his seat. By now the sky was blue, and a breeze was devouring the fog. Slogging through stale-smelling dirt, we reached the barn. Its door open, it was filled with mounds of decomposing straw.

When I spotted the familiar ash-wood stick and, a little further, a medium-sized mallet, all became clear.

Farther in, a gray-patterned blanket was spread out on the ground, still imprinted with the outline of a human body (or bodies). Dumbstruck, we stood around that blanket. A bird groaned in a tree, a bird that hadn't yet flown south, and perhaps didn't intend to. Minni took my arm. Greifer panted asthmatically.

"No tracks leading away?" I asked.

Greifer shook his head. "No. Fog. Rain. No."

After another silent spell he had made a decision.

"Help us, Minni—yell."

"What should I yell?"

"Call Lussi."

"Me?"

"Who else?"

"How should I call her?"

"The usual way."

Minni hesitated.

"Do it," I said stupidly. You can really get into humiliating situations. Sleepy, I was already deferring to Greifer.

"Lussi!" Minni's voice cracked as she called.

"Louder," Greifer hissed.

"I've lost my voice."

"Lussi!" Greifer ignored her complaint. "Louder!"

"Again."

"Lussi! Lussi! Luusssii!"

There was a faint echo: Lusssii-luussii . . .

By now the sun was pretty high up and the world looked a little safer.

As we stood at the door of the barn, I felt Minni's elbow poking me.

Following her gaze I spotted a small butterfly rising out of the darkness and briefly landing on a crossbeam. In my youth I'd taken an interest in entomology for a time. I changed my hobbies often. But that almost-white butterfly, with radial veins through its wings, looked familiar. The corners of its wings that were nearest to its body were tinted orange. Without a doubt, it was the dawn butterfly who was sitting above us—*Anthocaris cardamines*, a close relative of the cabbage butterfly.

The butterfly of the dawn sat still.

Unless it wasn't really the dawn butterfly . . . ? Who knows.

It took off into the blue of the sky.

Greifer hadn't seen it.

"Nothing here. Let's go." He led us back to his snoozing driver.

Later on I wondered aloud why Greifer had bothered with us. Minni thought that he was scared. Didn't have the guts to face such mysterious powers alone. But didn't he have some official protection he could call on? We didn't know. Possibly Greifer wanted to conceal as long as possible from his superiors—certainly he had superiors, everyone has superiors—the embarrassing fact that one of their own, namely Joosep, was now a vampire. Try as we might, we couldn't really guess how the powers-that-be might react to this information. The position of that gang of tyrants on the issue of vampires was ambivalent and unclear. It's extremely difficult to reconcile the rational and the irrational. I mean these words literally: my reader might get the impression that under the heading "irrational" I mean unreal, and under "rational" real—that vampires don't exist while Greifer does; that black magic doesn't exist while politics do—and, therefore, what connections could there be between them beside symbolic or allegorical ones? What I'm really trying to talk about, however, is how difficult it is, although tempting, to search for any kind of isomorphism between the known and the unknown. (Lacan proposed that reality is embodied unreality—it's difficult, as such, to imagine what has yet to be embodied; we don't even know what percent of unreality has been made real thus far, out of all the ambient unreality still out there.)

Maybe Greifer's billiard-ball head harbored similar thoughts that he would naturally never reveal to us (or to himself). Maybe he realized that if he openly admitted Michelson's existence, the Party would expel him for failing to adhere to the dictates of dialectical materialism.

Poor Greifer!

How could we help him? We could stand in for Joosep, whose mind was open, and who was familiar with vampires, at least through literature.

Which made him, after last night, all the more dangerous.

But Greifer, pretending to be manly, would not ask for our help.

Climbing into the car, he barked: "To the asylum!"

Minni began to giggle. "Thank you Greifer." Was she laughing or crying?

3

"Tiktus fell in a ravine, his guts spilling out," Renner told us willingly. "Ahva naturally was going to avenge him. Wait a second. I screwed up. Peetrus . . . I killed him with a single shot—or was it several? It doesn't matter. I also liquidated Luukus and Kroomis. My bullet went in one of Lopsi's ears and came out the other. And only after that did Tiktus fall in the ravine, yes, after my bullet had gone in one of Lopsi's ears and out the other, only then did Tiktus fall in the ravine with guts hanging out. Ahva naturally wanted to get revenge! On me! He was taking aim at me! But then came Teese, you see, Teese, and he liquidated Tiktus and Pianoor, bashing their skulls in, and Dumnus, Passus, and Riipus with his long beard. Muuleon then wanted to liquidate Teesus, but his bullet hit Krantor, God damn it . . ."

Renner drank some water. We were in Renner's room, with his doctor's permission.

"Since that time I've tried to be a good friend to Teese . . ."

"Because he saved your life?"

Renner nodded.

"But even earlier too, when Eurüüt betrayed . . . grabbed Potaamia."

"That far back?"

Renner nodded again. "We were brothers in arms."

Minni was taking notes as I had asked her to do. Renner noticed this and his talk became agitated. He was a vain man without much energy. His brow was covered in sweat.

"Aade will come . . . maybe today . . ."

"An idea, you said?"

"No, 'Aade'!"

"And where does he come from?"

"From the same place."

"And you know this Aade?"

Renner nodded. "Very well. I visited him with Teese."

He banged his fist on the table.

"We did!"

"Maybe you can tell us a little more about that visit?" Greifer suggested carefully.

But Renner sank back onto his pillow and closed his eyes.

We all exchanged glances and left him alone.

The Doctor was in his office.

"Yaah-haah," he sighed, offering us his sofa. His red-rimmed eyes glaring at us, he loosened his tie and grunted, "How about a little cocktail?"

Greifer shook his head. Minni too, and so what could I say, though my head was spinning and I could have used a drink.

The doctor shrugged and took a measuring glass from his cabinet.

"In that case I'll have one myself," he said, pouring out a slug and downing it.

After that he perked up.

"Well, what are your impressions?"

"He said that 'aade' is coming . . . did he mean 'idea'?"

"No! 'Aade'! Capital *A*. Aade!" the doctor declaimed with the kind of passion one usually reserves for personal problems. "That's the thing, it's Aade!"

He emptied another glass.

"I owe you an explanation, an *Erklärung*. Renner is a fascinating person. It's a shame to subject him to electroshock."

"So why do you?"

"It's necessary."

"But why?" Minni insisted.

"That's a good question," the doctor said admiringly. "A very good question. Because our society has no use for him the way he is. And I'm a servant of society. Perhaps it's demeaning for people to constantly be the objects of his peculiar scrutiny. But let me continue. Renner has broken with reality, *von der Wirklichkeit des Objektes* . . . and he lives in the world of mythology. For him our world is a contrivance, *Schein* . . . to him all human beings, animals, cars, vampires, and chairs are gods or demons. He sees a cupboard and thinks it's a god. *Gott*. An ordinary bat he takes for a creature out of Greek mythology . . . thinks it's a lamia. He fought in World War Two, which he takes for the battle between centaurs and Lapiths. Teese of course is Theseus. Renner has renamed every mythological creature, has discovered an intermediate form to overcome the discrepancies between his delusions and reality. So Theseus has become our first prime minister under the Soviets, his good friend. Now we're getting to the root of the matter. Together they went to Kronstadt in search of Koidula's grave, and they found it. They returned to Kronstadt in 1946 and took her remains to Tallinn to be reburied in Metsakalmistu, the Forest Graveyard. Renner was involved in all of that. And now gentlemen I'll tell you how Theseus and Pirithous journeyed into the underworld. The two were good friends and brothers in arms. Theseus, by the way, had tried to abduct the beautiful Helen when she was still young. And then . . ."

The doctor took a break. Wiped his brow, drained his glass, and went to his bookshelf. He wasn't wearing shoes—only socks. Having located what he was after, he came back to his desk, quickly refreshed his memory, closed the book, and sighed.

"Yes. This is how it goes." He became lively again. "Zeus, joking with them, said, among other things—ironically of course—why Pirithos (and Pirithos is Renner, remember that), why Renner, that is, excuse me, how come you haven't taken Persephone for your wife? Persephone or Proserpina being the spouse of Hades the ruler of the underworld, of course. Incidentally, Hades himself had abducted Persephone from the world of the living. Theseus and Pirithos—AKA Mr. Prime Minister and his Cultural Advisor, but let's stick with Pirithos and Theseus, at least for now, let's be consistent—so, yes, Theseus and Pirithos descended to the underworld to abduct Persephone. I hope you're following the plot. So yes, I felt it incumbent on me to inform you that Renner expects, in his own words, for Aades (that is, Hades) to appear tonight to avenge his abduction of Persephone."

"But, was this . . . abduction of Persephone successful, I mean in mythology?" I asked.

The psychologist put a finger across his lips.

"Sssh . . . That's our trump card. Renner doesn't remember a thing about the real world. He is *archaisch orientiert* . . . and we'll play that card when the time comes. So. No one for a cocktail?"

"I could use a drop," I said bravely.

"Great, I also could use a small one." The psychiatrist began mixing some liquids into his measuring glass.

After a taste of strong spirits, diluted with only a meager quantity of water, we went back to Renner together.

"We'll shake up Pirithos or Renner in a minute," the doctor promised. "And we'll see what happens when he *Empfindungen als von der Wirklichkeit total verschieden entdeckt.* When he understands that everything has changed. Just wait and see."

Renner was sitting on the edge of his bed, waiting for us.

"I hear you," he said pompously.

"Are you afraid of Aade?"

"Aade?"

"Are you scared or not?"

"Not much."

"He'll kill you," the doctor warned Renner. "He'll cut off your head. Stick a torch down your throat the way the centaur Rhoetus did to Euagroso the Lapith."

"Where did you hear about that?"

"These gentlemen with me are well informed."

Greifer nodded in confirmation.

After a while the doctor innocently asked, "So, what was it you did to Hades to make him mad at you?"

"I can't remember." Renner meekly bowed his head.

"Of course you don't remember. You have no memory!" the doctor roared like a lion. "But I'll remind you. You two went to abduct Prosperina, beg your pardon, Persephone, and Hades politely offered you a chair, but you chose the Chair of Oblivion. Later on, Herakles rescued Theseus—but you've been in the Oblivion Chair ever since, you damned amnesiac!"

The doctor began pacing.

"Because of that chair you've forgotten who Michelson is, and Koidula too." Then he added, casually, "But tonight you'll get to meet Michelson."

Renner sat still for a long time, his posture despondent.

The doctor blinked his eyes victoriously at us.

Renner now began to speak, his tone flat: "The parallels are not precise. Prime Minister Barbarus was no soldier, and certainly no Theseus. He was a modernist, futurist poet who lived in Pärnu. He made a living as a medical doctor. He never fought centaurs. Truly, he was *archaisch orientiert* . . . I can recite one of his verses: 'When the machine gun yelps like a dog that snarls at the end of his chain, baring his teeth at the approaching mastodon tank . . .'"

The doctor gave us a surprised look.

Meanwhile Renner continued dully, looking at the floor: "In the year 1939, Barbarus moved to Tallinn. Did he know that after the Russian invasion in 1940 he would be appointed prime minister? In any case he was a vain man, not that this should influence us negatively in appraising the value of his poetry . . . Barbarus! Yes, he was a constructivist, an anarchist too. He received the Stalin Prize in 1946, and that same year on November 29, he shot himself or was shot in his bathroom under mysterious circumstances.

"His real name was Vares, 'Crow,' an unsuitable name for a poet. 'Barbarus' means stranger—an alien, brutal, uneducated and ruthless. As prime minister he became Vares again. I remember that at Koidula's graveside in 1944, before her reburial, he said something like, 'Now that the heroic Red Army, together with the sons of Estonia, whose hands have now formed fists, under the leadership of the great Stalin, have liberated Estonia from German tyranny, only now can Koidula's words, "I want to rest, cast myself in your lap to dream, my holy Estonia," and her fondest hope, come true.' We took a ship to Kronstadt . . ."

"A regular ship?" I asked, not really knowing why.

Renner shrugged, looked up for a moment. Bowed his head again.

"I think so . . . And, by the way, before casting off, with the ropes already loose, a literary critic named Max Laosson jumped back onto the quay, saying that he had things to do. In 1949 he published an article that was instrumental in getting a number of popular authors thrown out of the Writer's Union, and whose works henceforth became forbidden. We stayed on board, though, and went home . . . How we struggled! I remember Lauter, the actor, the whites of his eyes sparkling like lightning . . . A blue-black wall of rain buried the contours of the city, the white cupola of the cathedral. Afterwards there was a banquet at Admiral Tributs's . . . vodka, caviar . . . now will you please leave me alone?"

We looked to the doctor. He nodded.

"Michelson won't show up before dark," he said to Renner from the door. "We'll be here to protect you."

Renner didn't even look up.

In his office the doctor launched into a little victory dance. "Did you see? Mentioning the Chair of Oblivion cured him!"

"I think he must have been sane all this time—just pretending to be sick," Minni ventured.

The doctor glared at Minni, then shrugged. "To hell with it, it's all the same. We need another cocktail."

Not waiting for a reply, he began clattering with his glassware.

Greifer cited Koidula to himself: "Till death I want to remember . . ."

The doctor corrected him: "Not remember but 'hold dear' . . ."

And he drank another glass down.

Minni added: "The odorous land of my fathers."

In the latest edition of Koidula's poetry, the word "odorous" always has an asterisk pointing the reader down to a note explaining that the word meant "scented" in the language of her time.

4

Later that day Minni and I took a walk in the asylum's park, marveling at the hideous clash of colors between the iridescent foliage and the mounds of long-abandoned and rusty cars. We spoke of our approaching marriage and the problems associated with it. Greifer, whose role in all this I could still only guess at, had delicately left us alone.

"The world's become so complicated, everything's topsy-turvy—with all the vampires and Greifers and Jooseps around, what's the point of getting married?" Minni asked.

"What could be better?" I countered. "We can certainly use the mutual support, and marriage seems to fit in nicely with all the other insanity."

The waning sunlight set the foliage ablaze. We were listening to the silence around us. Any traffic noise was far, far away. Even the asylum was silent.

I liked Minni a lot. She was beautiful and caring and I saw no reason to go digging around for some other woman. I hadn't even looked at another woman for a long time.

When I kissed her eyes, her eyelashes tickled my lips, and my involuntary squawk startled a few birds out of the bushes.

"Tonight is going to be rough," Minni prognosticated.

"You know what? I refuse to worry about it. Whatever happens will happen."

"Right you are," Minni said.

We pointed ourselves at the asylum, waiting on the hill behind the sunlit red-gold maple grove.

Meanwhile our doctor friend had put his medicinal spirits to good use. Nodding off on the sofa, he showed no interest in anything. His incomprehensible muttering encouraged us to leave him alone. We'd need him later.

I took a quick look at his small but decent library.

I read a few lines from Karl Jasper's *Psychopathology*, but it was much too erudite for me.

It was getting dark.

Greifer came in, gave the doctor a passing glance, shrugged, hung his leather coat on a hook, and checked the time.

Clearly the doctor wasn't going anywhere. We went to Renner on our own.

The man on the bed was staring at the ceiling.

We didn't want to disturb him. Actually, we didn't know what to say, so we didn't say anything. Minni arranged herself on a chair. I approached the window and looked out at the twilit park. Under the trees it was already night. Yellow leaves trembled in the treetops, some spinning to the ground. A few mental patients were still outside, hurrying in now to their nightly shelter. Then there were none.

Greifer stayed out in the hallway. Was he keeping watch? Well, it was up to him. Let him have his tactics and strategy.

What were we really waiting for?

Hades himself?

Who was Hades after?

And what did we have to fight him with?

We had Eastern European resignation, shattered illusions, a little intermittent enthusiasm, a cynicism born out of frequent foreign occupations, and the desire—like all long-isolated peasants—to better ourselves, somehow.

Michelson shouldn't underestimate us. After all, he was only a German Latvian who'd lived among the Russians.

Of course, he did have one advantage: immortality.

By now the park was completely dark. The glare of a search-light from a distant construction site blinded me.

We heard steps.

Greifer. He closed the door after him. Carefully.

It was a quarter past ten.

Renner still hadn't moved.

"If we really want him to come, shouldn't we turn off the lights?" Minni whispered.

Greifer shrugged, as though tired of all these irrelevancies.

"Will he show up at all in front of a crowd?" I asked. I also had my doubts.

"Herr Renner . . ." Minni approached the man on the bed. "Herr Renner, are you sure he'll come?"

Renner turned on his side.

Nodded.

Should I open the window or not? It would be a sign that someone was waiting. Wouldn't it be odd to wait for a visitor, then force it to ooze in through the cracks in the wall? But I didn't do anything. This alien world played by its own rules.

A sound: something had bounced off the window!

A moth. (You can't expect a dawn butterfly in the middle of the night.)

The moth, gray and featureless, clung to the window glass. I approached with uncertain steps. How should I address it? Moth, are you the forgotten man from Kronstadt? Or just an ordinary moth?

I inspected the creature closely.

After a few seconds it disappeared into the dark.

It was half-past ten.

Greifer was reading a newspaper. The asylum was quiet. The thought occurred to me that in this place sleep must be deeper than anywhere else. Here one seldom sleeps without drugs—sweet sleep and sweeter dreams. The air of the asylum was pregnant with dreams.

At eleven o'clock we heard steps in the corridor.

The doctor finally slept it off, I thought wearily. He'll come in with a hangover, irate, ready to gum up the works.

I noticed that Greifer had his arm in his breast pocket.

Apparently the meaning of immortality hadn't quite dawned on him.

Michelson was at the door.

Let's be precise: it was the same man I'd met in Leningrad by the *Aurora*.

Greifer stood straight.

Beside Michelson was an unremarkable—yet in the glare of the bare bulbs a quite remarkable-looking—woman in a black plastic overcoat, a dark shawl on her head. Her pale face contrasted with her too-red lips, but not unbecomingly so, and her striking eyelashes were dark. Michelson wore a dark, diagonally patterned overcoat and a soft fedora. He took off the hat. Renner stirred.

"Excuse me, where can I . . ." muttered Michelson, looking for a place to hang his hat. The ward had no coatrack. Greifer, who was nearest to Michelson, could do no better than take the hat from his outstretched hand. Michelson rewarded him with a nod—and there was Greifer, hat in one hand, and his other hand still in his breast pocket. Michelson acknowledged the rest of us with a slight bow, then approached Renner.

Renner began to ease himself off the bed.

Michelson put a hand on Renner's shoulder and pushed him back, then sat down beside him.

The woman at the door began to speak. Although her voice was low, she sounded like thunder.

"Are you aware that my unfortunate brother Leopold died in Petersburg in 1880, emotionally exhausted, destitute, and despised by all? He was buried in Preobrazensky Cemetery in an unmarked grave. We heard of his death many days after the fact. Our Estonian relatives showed no interest in their destitute relative. In the Old Folks' Home, Leopold had been a nobody, and he departed his miserable life isolated and scorned. Had we treated him as he deserved instead of according to the prevailing moral code of the day, it could have been different . . . But now he was dead and we couldn't even find his grave. For a week Eduard shuffled back and forth between Pontius and Pilate, obtaining the necessary documents, all the verbal and written information he could find, until he finally contacted the pastor of the Jesus Church and found the grave. We thought, let God give him the peace he did not find on Earth. We had a headstone and a cross put up on his grave so he wouldn't have to rest among the nameless . . ."

She took a break to wipe her brow.

"But I don't know exactly . . . I can't remember if our Estonian relatives contributed to the memorial . . . I do remember that Eduard promised to pay all the expenses if it came to that . . . but I don't know!"

Michelson dismissed her concerns. "Let's not speak of it. The past is past."

"But think of how unfair it was. You behaved so magnanimously, and yet to be treated the way you've been treated . . ."

"Peace, my dear, peace," Michelson interrupted her firmly.

He took a flat bottle from his breast pocket, unscrewed the cork, and took a swig. As he handed the flask to the woman, I could see a trickle of red at the corner of his mouth. He wiped it off, leaving a rusty stain on his white handkerchief. The woman took a sip, replaced the cork, and handed the flask back to Michelson, who stuck it in his coat.

Greifer suddenly threw Michelson's hat to the floor and left the room roaring like an asthmatic lion. We heard him cursing and slamming doors, then all was silent again. I opened the window on the snapping of branches below. Someone was on a rampage, began throwing up, and between spasms went on cursing in two languages. I couldn't tell who or what he was cursing at. After a while the sounds receded. A dog began to bark, desperately, attacking. There was a shot, then a whine. Silence descended on the park. There was only the distant city traffic, and now the whistle of a locomotive.

"I won't offer you any," Michelson patted his bulging breast pocket. "Tastes differ. Besides, for us it's a question of life, as you already know."

I closed the window.

Renner was on his feet sorting through his bedside table.

"Shall we go?" he asked over his shoulder.

"Where to?" asked Michelson.

"*Herr* himself must know that."

"You? You don't go anywhere."

Renner hesitated, a soap dish in hand. "We aren't going?"

"What we? Which we?" Michelson smiled. "Let's not quibble. It's not easy to call things by their proper names, I know. And who's to say what's proper? But Herr Renner, to put it bluntly, you seem to think I came here to eat you. Not so. We, both of us, came here to announce that we no longer touch humans. Where did the blood in my flask come from? A blood bank, naturally. We have contacts. Yes, we need blood to live, but we no longer infect anyone, at least not in this little country, this Estonia with its surfeit of suffering and its many dilemmas. Blood donors are anonymous. They can't be traced. Certainly I've done some terrible things. When I first came here, I made a number of mistakes. I went around as if in a fog. I bit the wrong people. I didn't care what I did. It was all the same to me. For me the entire country and all its people were guilty. A few little children, some fellow travelers in the night, someone called Poder. And then that false Lydia whose name was Lussi, I believe? An ugly story, but I, gentlemen, don't intend to be held responsible for it all. Neither will I go on apologizing forever. It wouldn't accomplish anything. Vampires and donors go back a long way. They're still with us today. I'm no exception. At least I'm aware of what I'm doing. Did I mention the blood bank? That's my supply. I don't drink much. But I do drink. I need it regularly."

He looked up at the woman, and she went to him. He put his arm around her waist.

"We live in the country, in the provinces. We do as much good as we can. We try not to break the law, in any case."

"Who's mad now?" asked Renner.

"You are, Herr Renner," replied Michelson icily. "That was decided long ago."

"All right," Renner agreed, "but why do you only drink blood?"

"In the first place, blood determines life or death," replied Michelson. "I must choose whether I am or am not, and—see how shameless I am—impertinently, I choose to be. And in the second . . ."

He smirked pretentiously.

"In the second place . . I like how it shocks people."

Meekly, he bent over.

The woman stroked his head.

"There's no need . . . Edushing . . . there's no need," we heard her whisper.

Michelson sobbed.

"I love you, have always loved you," she told him, "and I knew you would come back . . ."

"But you gave my ring to a stranger . . ."

"She stole it. Took it herself. I'm thirsty . . ."

"Want a sip?"

"Please . . ."

The woman reached for Michelson's pocket. They drank. Michelson dried his tears.

"You have just witnessed a tender domestic scene. What does it mean? Only that even immortals sometimes get a little tense."

Renner became agitated. "But why don't you take your revenge on me?"

"For what?"

"We dug up your grave . . . Barbarus and I . . . and afterwards the ship . . . I helped with the digging . . ."

Michelson dismissed him. "Let bygones be bygones. Now that we have a new perspective on life, now that we have a lovely homestead in a forest glen, with little feet running around . . . shouts of joy, happy babbling, and all that . . . I should be thanking you, Herr Renner, and through you the whole Estonian nation . . ."

"What I don't understand is what Lussi was guilty of," Minni interrupted.

"That girl? She wasn't guilty of anything. I'd only just arrived in Estonia then. Everything was new to me. I wanted to destroy everything, even Lydia—no matter which version of her I ran into. I wanted to destroy whomever I met. I confess, I was rather angry . . . Lussi was wearing Lydia's ring. And even without the ring . . . a beautiful maiden . . . a thirst for blood . . . *verstehen Sie?* After a while, though, I began to sober up, began to appreciate your struggles for freedom, your natural desire to conduct your own affairs, to be a free nation in a free land. Of course—I do need blood! That I won't deny. But, as I've already said at least three times—only from a blood bank! I no longer infect anyone."

"So you favor an independent Estonia?" asked Renner with, for him, unexpected earnestness.

"Yes," replied Michelson. "And because of that, we will make ourselves scarce. No one will have cause to complain about us."

The window clattered.

Someone was rattling the window frame.

A bat was beating itself on the glass.

Teeth bared, mouth open.

And persistent.

In awe and fear we watched that innocent yet maniacal creature.

After a while it flew away.

How long had it been there?

But when we looked around, Michelson was gone.

His lady companion as well.

No one saw them leave.

The door opened.

Our doctor, holding a hypodermic, was leaning on the threshold.

Who wants to be injected, he asked us with his eyes.

We said good night to everyone and left in a hurry.

The night was soaking wet, deserted, a world of ghosts and their kind. Rain was still sprinkling down. We walked through the asylum park to the gate. It was well past one o'clock. No more buses.

"At least now we're out of it," Minni said.

"Don't be so sure."

"He seemed sincere to me. Why else would he bother to come and talk to us? He could have eaten us in our sleep, sucked us dry. No, he has a soul! He went on and on because something was bothering him. He has regrets. At the same time, he was realistic . . . No, I don't believe that a human . . ."

Here she got stuck.

"Anyway, I can't believe that anyone could be that wicked," she convinced herself.

"What about that woman?"

"Who?"

"The one with him."

"You didn't recognize her?"

"No."

Minni thought it over for a while then shook me by my shoulder.

"That's right. You didn't go to Pärnu. Of course! You know who she was? Koidula, the Koidula who was there at the meeting, gathering, ceremony, whatever it was."

"But . . . How could she have been the real Koidula?"

"Dear, no more questions. My darling Joonatan, isn't it enough that between us we've now lived through events—horrible events—that an ordinary person would never even dream of?"

I had to agree with her.

5

But things were getting worse!

Pinned to our door was a letter.

And here it is:

Minni and Joonatan!

Perhaps my sadness was written in the stars, but it suits this departing soul and won't really surprise anyone. I just wanted to tell you that I'm leaving, but I don't plan to ramble on and on about it. I'm not going far. I met a young man who lives in Helsinki, and when we first met I never could have guessed at the deep feelings he would have for me. We met during a crisis, at least it was a crisis for me, since I'd just lost my humanity and had hurt many people, but this young man changed everything. He was like a vision for me. We talked a lot, among other things, about the problem of good and evil. You might not believe me: I used to be wicked and sick in my mind and

I thought that the way I was was the way I had to be. Thanks to this young man, however, I discovered how good it can be to be good. It's a matter of overcoming your animal instincts. Also, it suits me to distance myself from this battlefield we live in. I want to eat yogurt. It's so cheap in Scandinavia, where people eat it all the time, but here we can't produce it, just like we can't produce anything. And in Helsinki you can find all sorts of miracle doctors, my friend told me, like Ludmilla and Tamara and others. The air is cleaner there and at night the youngsters bark louder but they bite less.

I plan to return when I no longer feel wicked, or feel the seeds of sinfulness in my heart, and when you have begun to rebuild Estonia in a more positive way.

Regards to everyone,
Lussi
PS—Watch out for Joosep.

"What an odd day," Minni muttered. She was on the bed still wearing her dress from last night. "The enemy is capitulating and emigrating."

Yes indeed. The old vampires were retiring to a forest glen. Greifer had disappeared into the bushes in a panic, and now Lussi was off to Helsinki. What about us, Minni?

I was thinking aloud.

"We are what we are."

"Like mirrors that reflect, but produce nothing of their own?"

Like *a mirror carried along a road.* (Stendhal.)

"Minni, take off your dress. It's getting wrinkled. But consider this: if we, the mirrors, weren't around, there also wouldn't be anyone to reflect. Things happen because of those who observe."

"That's too complicated for me," Minni said as she wriggled out of her dress. "But you were talking about mirrors. Those creatures from the other side don't show up in mirrors. Last night I was thinking of turning my back to Michelson to put some lipstick on and check whether I could see him behind me in my hand mirror. But that bat appeared and Michelson vanished almost as soon as the idea occurred to me."

"You could have tried to reflect the bat."

"I'll reflect you in a minute," Minni threatened. She hadn't even bothered to pull the blanket over her.

"OK. Let's see your reflection."

I brought her a hand mirror.

Suddenly I felt queasy.

She reflected.

Began to snore.

Her hand and the mirror dropped onto the blanket.

Her hair, lips, and breasts all sagged a little in sleep.

I dreamt I was sleeping the last sleep by that sleeper, with my heart stopped and my cheek frozen against hers. (Emily Bronte, *Wuthering Heights*.)

6

The following day, rumors were already circulated about the first casualties.

Greifer had hanged himself.

There was some logic to that.

He'd been much too smug.

He wore a leather coat and his head was like a billiard ball.

People like that are liable to have sudden breakdowns.

Minni and I didn't grieve for long.

Actually, I can't say that we grieved at all.

Our acquaintance with Greifer had been fleeting.

We were busy furnishing our home.

I happened to recall that in Bram Stoker's *Dracula* there's an anti-vampire professor named Van Helsing.

Joosep, whom we were warned about, never showed up.

The trees were bare of leaves.

Organic life went on as usual, behind the scenes.

VIII

And what have you been up to in the meantime?
—From private papers

MORE SYNCHRONIZED EVENTS

1

That peasant whom we know casually and will never get to know better—readers were warned about that at the beginning of this novel—now regularly wakes at dawn instead of sunset. One morning he even beat the sun, since autumn had come and farmers get going pretty early anyway. He opened his eyes, came back to earth, looked around, and saw nothing. "What is darkness?" he mused. "Does it only mean that I can't see, or does it mean that there's nothing to be seen?" He couldn't decide. "But I know something is there. When I get up and reach out my hand I'll find my pants on that chair." He reached out and found his pants. He put them on and turned on the light. Later, he realized that he should have turned on the light first. But it was no big deal! What happened, happened. Tomorrow I'll be smarter. He fed his pigs and his dog. He knew nothing of Joosep. But we can assume that a few years later, Joosep, on his way to Riga, secretly spends a night in this peasant's barn. He wakes before the rooster and blithely continues on his journey.

2

The wife, whose husband and children were no longer at their grandmother's, and who therefore was no longer alone in her house, heard no one at all at her door. One of her daughters was playing in the kitchen. She ran to her mother all of a sudden, shouting cheerfully: "Look mama, my hand is red with berry juice!" It was blood, actually, since she'd been playing with razorblades. She was three years old. Mother, concealing her alarm, quickly dressed the wound.

Her husband was watching TV and knew nothing about it.

Joosep will never appear in this neighborhood. He will never ring her doorbell.

What fortunate children.

3

The young wife with a cheating husband saw Joosep standing by her bed one lonely and sleepless night. He said, "Woman, are you thirsty?"

He took a knife, cut his breast, grabbed her by the hair, pushed her mouth against his chest, and forced her to suck.

She became a vampire.

Joosep warned her: "Keep this to yourself. Don't breathe a word of this to anyone. When our time comes, I'll send word."

She kept his secret.

4

Renner repeated, mechanically and dutifully, as if he was counting sheep:

Ammpüks killed Ehheekles, Makaarius killed Erituub, I killed Küümel, Mopsus killed Tiites, Käänus killed Elüümus . . .

That's as far as he got.

The next morning he was found in a pool of blood with a twisted neck and broken spine.

Was Joosep capable of perpetrating such a meaningless act?

Did he have a sense of humor?

Was this absurd murder part of some grand plan?

If only we knew!

What's Joosep aiming at? Should we believe all the rumors?

5

He was said to have reached the island in the early morning, before the breeze had scattered the fog. Some say he came in a motorboat, others say in a dinghy, but it was probably a motorboat.

Almost certainly in a motorboat, conceivably in early October on a cold and rainy day, with a nasty fog blanketing a smooth sea—maximum visibility fifty meters. He must have been concerned about finding his target. So he had peered into the fog, waited, and lo, a big dark something was looming ahead and getting darker all the time. Soon it was clear he'd reached an island, monochromatic in the fog that had washed away all colors. He stopped the motor and waited for his prow to hit the beach. It was said he didn't leave the boat right away but crouched there on his seat for a time. Was he reviewing his plans or was he lost in his memories? Who knows?

Meanwhile the breeze had risen: waves were lapping against the boat. So, either a lot of time had passed or just a little, there's no way for us to be sure, but he must have stood up and stepped over the gunwale, and grimaced in the cold water that came up to his knees. He waded ashore and looked around.

(I know this island. One day at dawn we were leaving the island along a narrow ridge, the same ford by which we'd come. This rise was anything but straight, but when we'd come in, the sea had never reached over our waists.)

This time, however, the sun was in our eyes, and we couldn't see the bottom, and we lost our way. We were in our teens and we had food with us that had been prepared by our parents. We lifted our bags over our heads. We were confused—it seemed like the seabed had changed overnight and we would never get home. We had to spend the brief summer night by a campfire on the island.

Who with? My whole class, since it was a class trip. The evening was warm, and our fire warmed it more. Most of us went to sleep before dawn. I stayed up, but I can't remember who with. Probably a woman—a girl, I mean. I remember we took a trail that ran around the island. There was a hillock in the middle of the island with a few juniper bushes that prevented our friends from seeing us, though we could still hear their voices. I remember the orange glow in the sky just before dawn, an orange ball out in the gray that married the sky to the sea. And how cold it became! But her I don't remember at all. After we sloshed in the shallows for a good hour we finally reached the mainland.

So the island that Joosep landed on that morning was no stranger to me. Hearing the rumors, I could picture the island in my mind's eye. His pants and shoes were dripping wet. Naturally he stepped out of the water, took them off, wrung and hung them on a juniper bush to dry.

His thighs and shins were covered in goose bumps. He waited for the sun to rise and bring some warmth. An hour went by and I can't say what thoughts passed through his head. This island now belonged to him. Without even bothering to check, he was sure he was the only one there. Here, away from people, in almost perfect isolation, à la Robinson Crusoe, the only thing that could have unnerved him would have been if the island had begun to float away, like a bundle of reeds in a flooded river. We know there are such things as bog islands with no anchoring roots, and we've read about the floating islands in the Sargasso Sea. Still, I doubt if such things ever crossed his mind. He'd been squatting and leaning his cheek on his hand. Meditating, probably. People today have very few opportunities for solitude, especially people who have to depend on others.

The sun came up. Squawking seagulls flew over the island. Despite the world now appearing more accommodating, Joosep still crouched gloomily in his chosen spot. Why should the sun make me happy? he might have thought. Still, he was stoical about his situation. The world has its rules: a bit on the vulgar side, but so what? His pants were drying off, there was a coast guard helicopter on the horizon—too far for its noisy engine to have bothered him—the juniper berries were ripening, and the sun would keep on rising, what else could it do?

The sun may make us mortal, but that's the only harm it does.

Don't always believe the movies.

At noon he put on his mostly dry pants and ate his sandwiches. Everyone swears the sandwiches were cheese. What does it matter? Some people get so preoccupied with minutiae they miss what's important. They look at the cheese and not at the sea, its play of colors, its moods and its changes, its divine and earthly margins, its influence; its meaning to fish and fishermen; its indifference to the widow of a sailor. What does a sandwich matter beside all that complexity?

Equal to the occasion, Joosep indulged in a little ironic self-pity. His scabrous lips whispered, "Where's the palm tree that's supposed to grow on my desert island to provide shade for me until a monster squid, a favorite subject for cartoonists, appears out of the sea? And where is the shark that speaks, and why don't I have my favorite books with me, anything but the Bible, let's have some Montague Summers, and why isn't the *Lord of the Flies* buzzing around me?"

That's what he was supposed to have muttered, and giggling silently.

Then he closed his eyes and slept.

The sea spoke louder. For a while the clouds hid the sun.

The island was twenty kilometers west of the mainland. The other side of the island faced the open sea, and beyond the sea was unseen Sweden. Of course, not mainland Sweden, since first there's Gotland, which the Estonians call Ojamaa. Estonians have historical ties with Gotland. Some Swedes of this generation are surprised to hear that east of the Baltic Sea there are Estonians. They believe that on the eastern shore live Sea Lions, Russians, Basques or God knows what else.

Considering the way things are with us right now, it's not such a bad guess.

Did Joosep dream?

For example: of a black cat pulling the hairs out of Joosep's beard? One by one? Meanwhile, on a podium in the background, an orchestra of mice dressed in tuxedos plays Strauss. Mama mouse, let's call her Josephine, sings the following song:

> How interesting to walk with a band,
> Knapsacks on our backs and a teapot.
> The setting sun, no longer blinding hot,
> Looks down the wide trails of our land.

These old-time propaganda/marching songs, with their sublime melancholy, can really cast a spell over an unwary writer. I could be mistaken, of course, as to what the mouse sang, but then it's never easy to establish the truth after the fact, and it may not even be necessary.

Anyway, now the mice are singing Dunayevsky's "March of the Young Naturalists," which is not a nature-philosophical poem, not at all. The lyricist was thinking more about those amateur nature lovers who carry out various observations and gather climatic data on flora and fauna (but not on humans, God forbid!) in their spare time. The members of the mouse orchestra sing the chorus and Josephine sings solo. Dressed in black she stands before a red satin curtain. Meanwhile the cat is still busy with the dreamer's beard. He pulls and pulls and doesn't make a sound. Then something else happens: the dream changes location, but on waking, this part can't be recalled. The cat might have changed into a dog, the mice might have turned into cows, or some cows into more mice, but at the last moment, with all hope gone, reality reappeared and saved the day.

Where am I?

I'm on an island, on my own island.

Later, after noon, he gathered snail shells, but getting bored, chucked them all into the sea. Then, it seems, a boat motor starting up was heard. This time, before wading back to the boat, Joosep had wisely pulled off his pants. Then, standing up to pull his pants on again, the boat rocked dangerously—but this is another irrelevant detail. What matters is that the engine started and the boat began to move, leaving behind a foamy wake, speeding now to a spot in the water where a periscope was rising from the deeps.

The island was empty again. Insects flew along their invisible air lanes, undisturbed, until a shadow slid over the island—a large bird that gobbled up the bugs in her mouth, her beak I mean, just the way the fishermen sing:

Im Sudden / In the south

Auf einer Insel reich an Zimt und Öl / There was an island rich with cinnamon and oil

Und edlen Steinen die im Sande glitzern / And precious stones glittering in the sand

Ein Vogel war dere wenn am Boden Fussende glittere / A bird came along

Mit seinem Schnabel höher stamme Krone / And picked up something in its beak

Zerpflucken konnte / From the crown of the tree.

If we're to believe Stefan George, anyway.

Soon the bird found an abandoned sandwich wrapper and she shook it in her beak for a long time, until the wind carried the shredded paper out to sea. In addition we might say that the evening became cloudy and stormy, but that's also irrelevant. Someone else can tell that part of the story.

And by that time Joosep was long gone.

6

Anderson, the thief, now a respectable merchant, arrived not in Kaunas but in Riga.

Even before he turned down the first street he came upon, he wondered: Who's waiting for me around this corner?

It's a favorite subject for cartoonists. It could be a man with a club, a mother-in-law with a rolling pin, a Beijing Palace lion, or who knows what. Naturally, in a strange city, the corner will probably reveal a strange landscape, a strange street. There could be a white horse there, or steps leading down to a river that can be seen only after rounding the corner. And when we do round the corner, we'll cease to exist for those who stay behind. We drop below the horizon, fall into a black hole. Only sound might reveal something about our fates—when we shriek, for instance, it might be thought that we were startled by something, but that could as easily be incorrect, since we might just shriek to tease those who stayed behind, which is not at all an uncommon thing to do. Let's not dwell on it. When we've rounded the corner we'll find out what's there. But let the others go first—we'll stay on this side. It's nighttime in a strange city. We've arrived by train, and we know that first we'll go straight ahead across a road, then across a small square, then along an avenue to the next cross-street. We're following directions. The streets are empty. Only the wind blows, just the way it did when we were young. We've reached that next cross-street. We look around, just in case, and put down our suitcase, as if to rest. Beside us is a stucco house with its windows dark. And beyond the house is our cross-street, the house being on the corner. How long are we supposed to wait? We pick up our suitcase and proceed. Our gut tells me something is wrong. Our blood begins to congeal in our veins. Fortunately our soft shoes are quiet. Creeping closer to the corner, we find our apprehension justified: around it, the elongated shadow of a man falls on the sidewalk in front of us. Its head longer than normal, also its neck and chest . . . the lower body remains hidden. This shadow waits, unmoving. Doesn't this idiot realize that his shadow has given him away? Does he think we're still so dopey from our long journey that we can't notice a few details? He's mistaken. We see everything. We stand still and he stands still. It's past midnight, and only a few blocks away our friends are waiting for us. Better to go around this obstacle. And so we retreat, slowly at first, very quietly, then faster, still facing the corner, eyes on that unmoving shadow. Eventually our nerves break and we run. We run and run until we find a cab that will take us to our friends. After a casual conversation we go to sleep between clean white sheets. Through our closed eyes we still see that fixed shadow on the corner. We're happy to feel regular heartbeats pulse in our ears. In the morning we attend some political meeting. True, we don't really participate. Lots of nuances remain unappreciated. In any case, we side with the people, not the government. We feel grateful for the instinct that told us to look down, to look at the sidewalk by the corner of the street just a few blocks from our safe haven.

So much for Anderson.

7

The city types who went to the country to make money, thus forming a friendly little group, had by the autumn dissolved once more into separate individuals. They no longer interest us.

Still, rumor has it that the dear old woman, the one who was despondent over a fox stealing her chickens, has since become a vampire.

We don't have any proof, but have you ever tried to squeeze toothpaste back into the tube?

8

It's a shame I didn't get to know Alli better. A wonderful girl and a lively one, always ready for such audacious tasks as protecting the traces of a prehistoric meteorite crash from bulldozers. In these difficult times for our nation she certainly deserves a place of honor. Good luck to her and good health! Should we never meet again, regards to everyone!

9

The upstanding and righteous old man who worried so much
about law and order in Lasanmäe eventually became recon-
ciled to my living with Minni. I suspect he still yearns for
Lussi, but try to catch a bluebird.

One day, eating his supper, the old man read the following
article in a journal:

"Vampire bats have no place in authentic Estonian folklore. However, there is an old belief that the bat was originally created by Vanapagan, the traditional devil figure of the
Estonians. Vanapagan is not the Christian devil but a clumsy,
good-natured, sly trickster; a synthesis of Christian and sha-
manic beliefs. Vanapagan plays practical jokes but avoids doing any serious harm. Another myth has it that bats are actually
creatures of God. A bat was thought only to suck the blood
of white animals, and even to attack humans when they, to be
seen at night, venture outdoors wearing white clothing. This
uncommon event was recorded in the district of Kuusalu. The
factuality of the bat-as-vampire was confirmed by the discov-
ery of real blood-sucking bats in South America in the sev-
enteenth century. Their scientific designations are *Desmodus*,
Diaemus, and *Diphylla*. They are indeed a danger to animals.
Their saliva kills pain and at the same time thins the victim's
blood. Vampire bites measure about five millimeters wide by
five millimeters long. The vampire bat can lap up about twenty
milliliters of blood in half an hour. Without blood these bats
can only live for about three days, though on the second dry
day they begin to shrivel. In Mexico (according to unverified
data), vampires kill around fifty thousand cows and ten thou-

sand horses every year. It's worth adding that the bite of these vampires can transmit rabies. Some well-meaning researchers claim that vampires never attack humans, but other researchers contradict them. Wallace, one of the forefathers of Darwinism, contended that some people are especially vulnerable to vampire bites. Explorer Percy Fawcett described how vampires sedate their victims before they attack by vibrating their wings monotonously. Vampires are a favorite subject in horror books and films. Attitudes toward vampires vary greatly culture to culture. They are especially honored in the literatures of Australia, Bosnia, England, Poland, and Sarajevo, while they are symbols of death in Ireland, India, Alabama, and Salzburg. In Southeast Asia and China they represent the forces of darkness. Vampires are *yin* creatures, feminine and shadowy; yet at the same time the *yin* is necessary to a long and happy life. Estonian superstition claims that a bat, especially its blood, is an aphrodisiac. 'After you catch a bat, take it to an ants' nest and let the ants eat away all its flesh. On its back the bat has a bone the ants won't touch. One end of the bone forms a hook, the other end a fork. When you want a boy or a girl to fall in love with you, walk past them slowly and touch their clothes with the hook end of the bone, but make sure they aren't aware that you're doing it. They will follow you. If you get tired of that person, touch their clothes with the forked end of the bone.' The bat also comes in handy in getting rid of an incubus. It seems that in Estonian folklore, the bat is a protector and talisman, not just a symbol for malevolence.

Because bats appear at twilight (about an hour after sunset, or just before dawn) people regard them as being creatures of two worlds—neither of the day nor of the night, being neither mice nor birds. And since they tend to inhabit ruins and caves and other gloomy places, they are often associated with melancholy. For a long time bats were thought to be entirely blind. Eventually it was discovered that bats locate their targets by sound (echo location), and that they can hear ultra-high frequencies.

In our climate bats sleep seven months out of a year, from October to April. They are conditioned to hibernate: if a sleeping bat is taken to a warm room during its dormant period, it can die in a few hours. Not all bats spend their winters here—many fly to warmer climates such as Central Europe. It has not yet been discovered whether they migrate singly or in groups, but identification by tagging has proven that this exodus takes place.

"I've only ever seen bats in flight," related one man when questioned about bats in his area. "Most likely it was in spring, and naturally after sunset—they flew like bullets through the branches of an apple tree that still had no leaves. I heard the rustle of their wings. My father told me they were bats. But I've never seen them in caves and bell towers. This isn't hard to explain. I don't really seek them out. Only a scientist would crawl into a cave in the middle of the winter to see some bats. A normal person avoids such places in any season. Think about it: you buy a ticket, ride for hours, slosh through the snow, crawl into a cave, breathe, listen, turn on your flashlight, find a bat, then wake the creature up (which can take almost an hour, and meanwhile the bat will have plenty of opportunities to bite you, and on top of that, let's face it—waking the animal up in the first place is sadistic and senseless), then sit and stare at a groggy bat for a while, learning what? Then you turn off your flashlight, crawl out of the cave, cross the field that's under new wet snow, hang around in twilight waiting for the bus that's at least half an hour late, and later on at home boil water to make yourself some tea to keep away the catarrh—all this takes a pretty fanatical devotion to the subject, as far as I'm concerned. No thank you. I have a family to take care of. So, in all honesty, I can't say I know much about bats. I've only ever seen them in flight."

Everyone has a right to his or her own opinion. Even this fellow. We shouldn't reproach him.

So: Although it's true that a bat can accidentally get itself tangled in the fluffy hairdo of a society woman, it makes no sense to involve them in human affairs. Just keep the following in mind: Bats have been on earth for millions of years, cats like to eat bats when they catch one, and the blood of a bat cures madness. You never know when this information might come in handy, perhaps in one of those awful silences when you and your beloved are trying to talk through the problems in your relationship, and neither of you can think of anything to say.

Bats are only a tiny part of the great mosaic of life we are doggedly trying to assemble.

SEE ALSO

Caras, Roger A. *Dangerous to Man.* Penguin Books, 1978.

Leach, Maria, ed. *Funk & Wagnalls Standard Dictionary of Folklore, Mythology and Legend.* Harper San Francisco, 1984.

What did our old man make of this article?

Nothing.

By the way, Minni and I passed under the old man's window while he was reading.

We walked by happy and in love and we intended never to give up that state of mind.

10

The unimportant person:

"We could call him Traaküla. Everyone would catch on pretty quickly that this is *Dracula* written the Estonian way. But this would be much too comic. Traaküla and Dracula! The story would turn into a parody, totally unsuited to a people who have been laboring for so long under the yoke of foreigners. Notwithstanding all our cynicism, can't we be serious for at least a few hours a day? Should we call him Jüri Rummo instead? He was a nineteenth-century horse thief and hero of the peasants—and so popular that his story was made into an operetta. He stole from the Baltic Barons who ruled over us, thinking we were all uncouth peasants. We could steal his name. But let's not. That would be cheating the public. Yes."

IX

From here on we can't rely
On anything that's indispensable.
—Michael Butor

FROM HISTORY

Everything's been so strange lately.

At times it all feels like a dream.

We're used to thinking of the vampire as an individual who ignores external influences, who follows his own star, lives and dies alone, that is, its own god or devil, speaks in solitude to its own conscience or other self, creates its own ambiance, eats only what it likes: a vampire's phone doesn't often ring, women avoid him because his lips are too red and he has bad breath, and this is why vampires hardly ever have any children to be taught the ways of their parents—or else to be warned against the ways of his parents. Vampires are thought to be loners.

And yet, sometimes these loners do join together.

And not only do they join forces, they launch counterattacks on society, refusing to sell their goods and even resorting to terrorism and burning down our buildings. We've tried to isolate the vampires and break down their resistance—all the more since they've begun to organize themselves into spy rings determined to sabotage our air-conditioners, devise cover-ups, and set things on fire! Their aim is to prevent our material progress. At one time they were uprooted and expelled from our country—but we neglected to destroy their bases on our soil. Our humane measures did not suffice. Finally, all those who had been insisting that the vampires be treated compassionately changed their tactics. Old methods of coping with the bloodsuckers were abandoned. Now the aim was complete eradication, expropriation, and confiscation of their assets. The bloodsuckers caught on too late to save themselves.

All this sounds somewhat cold and remote. Let's move from figurative bloodsuckers to real ones. Metaphors have their rightful place in literature, but that's all. Karl Marx's *Das Kapital* states: "Capital is dead labor, that, vampire-like, only lives by sucking living labor, and lives the more, the more labor it sucks." But political economics are better understood by making comparisons. Metaphors spread roots everywhere, but in the end they don't mean much.

Let's consider Uganda in East Africa, an ex-British Protectorate that became self-ruling on October 10, 1962, thus embodying the process the communists called "disintegration of the capitalist system." The first African ruler of Uganda was the one-time king of Buganda *kabaka* Mutesa II. In 1966,

Milton Obote, leader of Uganda's only political party, pushed him off the throne. Obote, naturally, suppressed all opposition, and Mutesa had to leave the country. In 1969 Obote proclaimed that all differences between the rich and the poor must be erased. In 1970 all the banks were nationalized and the so-called progressive order was instituted. In 1971, Idi Amin seized power in Uganda. He exiled all Jews, Asians, and Europeans. His slogan was that wealth belongs to the people. The economy of the country was soon in ruins. For a long time the Soviet Union was Idi Amin's ally. We sent him tanks and Kalashnikovs and he sent us coffee. He murdered hundreds of thousands of his people. They say he was a cannibal who practiced the blood rituals of his clan (the Kakwa). They say he would request to be left alone in a room with his victim. When pressed for time he would stab his victim with a knife and lap up the victim's blood. That was supposedly the Kakwa ritual. In 1976, at a social gathering, he blithely declared that human flesh was salty, saltier than leopard meat (See Henry Kyemba, *State of Blood*, 1977). And these horrible deeds weren't even the only reasons for Idi Amin's eventual fall from power. His troops invaded Tanzania, starting a war that ended with his defeat in 1979. Ruined in Uganda, he became an honored guest in Saudi Arabia.

Another cannibal was Emperor Bokassa of Central Africa, who also lost power in 1979, the same year as Idi Amin. Bokassa did away with his country's parliament, schools, banks, industry, and agriculture. He took personal command of the army and secret service. He was voted (?) the head of the country's only political party and its politburo for life. He controlled every communal organization in the country.

He personally executed children. Like Idi Amin, Bokassa supposedly had freezers filled with human flesh and blood. With France's aid he was dethroned along with all those who had sworn allegiance to him, and who had attempted to do away with, air-conditioners, TV sets, and libraries, and were, like their boss, drinkers of blood. Like their leader, they were overdue for liquidation.

So, how should the Africans have guarded themselves against these vampires? There's an intriguing method that comes to us from Poland, which at first glance seems to exploit a peculiarly vampiric brand of naiveté. Some old men recommend that you scatter kernels of grain around the building you want to protect, especially around its doors and windows. If a vampire arrives, it can't help but to count every last grain; the entire night passes in this way, and at dawn the vampire has to return to its grave.

But what if this sort of thing doesn't do the job? Then commando units have to be formed to go out and hunt vampires by night. The bloodsuckers must be forcibly torn away from their unholy work and told to gather their most needed possessions—they'll only be given a few minutes to do this—before being loaded onto trucks and driven to a ship or a ferry. It's well known that vampires dislike seawater, salt being a good disinfectant. Now they're shipped off to a deserted island. In the Middle Ages, some of the smaller Mediterranean islands were earmarked for just this purpose. But everything has its limits: when the islands get overcrowded, all the screaming might disturb the tourists on a passing cruise liner. To prevent copulation it's recommended that separate colonies be established for male and female vampires. Then the vampires can't multiply and will eventually die out. It sounds prettier in

English than in Estonian: *The Deportation of Vampires to the Tiny Islands of the Mediterranean*!

Now let's take a look at things from a different point of view.

A VOYAGE TO A DESERTED ISLAND:
CAPTAIN'S REPORT

At the time I had no idea that the plan was to get rid of all the bloodsuckers at once. The plans were top secret. Why should they let us know what was going on? We were unreliable. And maybe we deserved that reputation—I don't know. Life had become so complicated and unsettling in those days. In any event, I must repeat: We were kept ignorant of all their plans.

As for myself, I had been sailing those straits for years. My ship, the *Ümera*, had too much draft for the shallows there. During the terrible northern blizzards, when a good master wouldn't even put his dog out, the huge waves in the Hari Strait would have made the *Ümera* scrape bottom, lose headway, and capsize.

There was no way of estimating how big the waves in the Hari Strait would be, since the Baltic Sea couldn't be seen from the harbor. On days when we were reluctant to cast off, the brass would accuse us of sabotage. We needed discipline, they said, and waved their guns around. We had to obey. At first everything was okay, and my superiors enjoyed their moral victory, but when we reached the Hari Strait and met the Baltic Sea, the *Ümera* began to roll and they were all puking over the rail. Of course, they would never admit to being wrong, but at least there was no more talk of sabotage.

That's how it was in the straits.

In March I was told to report back to work. This was odd, since official navigation hadn't yet started up again after winter. The straits were still ice-bound and the navigation buoys were all in storage. But orders were orders. At first we just sat and waited in the harbor. As usual, we were kept completely in the dark. Finally an officer consented to give us a brief explanation. He said that when the passengers arrived, we shouldn't talk to them. We nodded our heads, shrugged to ourselves, and waited. The day was sunny and windless.

The passengers came escorted by armed guards and were immediately taken below. A few women carried infants. We recommended they make use of the sofa in the saloon. Some of the men wouldn't give up their seats. But on board a ship, the captain is next to God, so after a brief tussle the women were comfortably seated.

Then we sailed. There was no wind: no crying, moaning, or puking. Young girls took to singing on the bow. I wondered for a long time about who these people could be and why they had to be taken to an uninhabited island so far away. By this time I had been permitted to open my sealed orders. I was convinced it was a miscarriage of justice. For example, those singing girls were beautiful, and I just couldn't imagine them being guilty of anything. And those mothers with their suckling infants, what could they possibly have done? But it was forbidden to ask. We were about to cross the Styx, but with whom and why?

The day waned. The sun set. After a few days we were quite a long way north. At night the aurora borealis flashed in the sky. Many prisoners, unable to sleep, came up on deck to see the wonderful sight.

After spotting our first ice floes, we made our way with great caution, since we discovered that our radar wasn't working properly. Here and there huge icebergs floated past us.

A woman prisoner yelled, Look, polar bears!

We squinted, trying to spot the bears in the polar brightness, but saw nothing but whiteness. Had the bears already left? Or had the woman seen a ghost? This happens often in the high latitudes.

We had some drinking water left but nothing for washing or shaving. I feared that if the journey took much longer we would begin to lose our humanity—externally at first, and then internally. Suddenly

[The Captain's story breaks off here.]

MY POINT OF VIEW

I've flown over that area.

It so happened I once had the opportunity to visit New York. There's plenty of everything there, at least for the visitors. I had some interesting experiences in New York, but more of that some other time.

About my return flight: The airport check-in line was appalling. All sorts of athletes and playboys with electronic gadgets were in line ahead of me. I wanted a cigarette but it turned out that smoking was forbidden. And yet the smoke shop was still open! Reminded me of Moscow. After a quick whisky with Andres I found my seat on the plane. The day was waning. I couldn't sleep. An attendant announced that in four hours we'd have a brief stopover in Gander. I had no idea what Gander was. Everyone else seemed to know. They nodded their heads wisely. I didn't dare to ask anyone—all the Russians on board were well dressed. I gave a mental shrug—what good would it do me to know? After my demanding day I managed to fall asleep, and I woke to the announcement that in half an hour we would be landing in Gander. This made me happy—we'd already come a long way, maybe we even were halfway to Europe. But where was Gander? Not in Ireland—the airport there is called Shannon. Where else? Scandinavia? I didn't dare hope we'd come that far. Greenland? While I was speculating, we landed. No lights. Must be a transit airport, I thought. While we were walking to the passenger terminal, a blizzard was blasting away outside. Which country, which state was this? The merchandise for sale in the terminal was like any other merchandise, the Pepsi there like any other Pepsi. After a while I spotted a map on the concourse wall. A brief look confirmed my worst fears: we were in Canada, on the island of Newfoundland. My God, we had flown four hours and hadn't even crossed the Atlantic yet! I cringed until the boarding call came. We fastened our seatbelts. In inky darkness, snow was blowing. Jung has a concept: *Nachtmeerfahrt* (Night-sea-journey). I'd read about it but now I understood. I didn't see the Atlantic Ocean begin beneath us. How far below, how deep? I stared out of the window. The moon was out, but the aurora borealis was most prominent. How it rioted! Below us there was nothing, my subconscious told me: ignore it. Then—I thought I could see some icebergs. In the icy soup I could also see some ships, their lights bouncing off the water. Like june bugs. Who was manning those ships, what were they thinking about? Were they prepared for the worst? And still the aurora borealis flared on . . .

Soon the sky brightened, the sun appeared. At two o'clock at night! Of course, we were flying east! My gloom disappeared.

ANOTHER NEW YORK MEMORY

Jonas, the stage director, the Lithuanian immigrant (you may recall the strange incident with the taxi and the apparition on the side of the road?) told me one morning:

"Listen, I need some blood, badly."

I had a good laugh at this, but he insisted: he needed blood. All right then, we went out to get some. It was around ten o'clock on a rainy April morning, the temperature around forty degrees, and with a lot of wind coming off the sea. All of a sudden Jonas was in a hurry. We took a cab that soon got stuck in traffic. Jonas decided that the driver was incompetent, that he'd taken the wrong street, and so he started cursing at him, and the driver, a black man, started cursing him back. After a pointless fifteen minutes, Jonas yelled: "To hell with this. Let's walk!" And he jumped out of the cab. We had to run to get to his appointment on time. We carried umbrellas, but so did everyone else, causing countless collisions of umbrellas. All we heard was, Sorry! Sorry! Sorry! It was a full morning. I kept on walking into puddles. Soon my socks were soaked.

Our target was a Mr. Kelly's office on Second Avenue, ten blocks away. We ran all the way, as already mentioned.

At last we found the building and we stared at the foyer directory.

"No Kelly here," my friend said, despondent. "Let's try the next building," I suggested, but then I spotted Kelly's name after all. We took the elevator to the sixth floor, where women behind a glass wall were making wigs. Kelly himself was in the bathroom and appeared after a few minutes. My friend explained that he needed blood for costumes, but that it had to be washable. Kelly nodded and dug out a container the size of a beer bottle. My friend removed the cork and tested the blood with his finger. It looked real. "But will it wash out?" Jonas asked pointedly. Kelly, an honest man, shook his head sadly and said, Not completely. My friend explained that he couldn't afford new costumes for his murdered actors and actresses every performance. Kelly understood the situation but couldn't help us. He suggested mixing shampoo in with the juice, but this was old news to Jonas. We said a friendly good-bye to Kelly and left. Jonas said that Kelly's blood juice would be okay for the movies but not for the stage. Out on Second Avenue the rain had let up and all the umbrellas were folded. I tried to console Jonas. He just shrugged. "Why settle for Kelly," I asked. "Who else is there?" he asked in reply. Leapfrogging the puddles, we headed for Broadway. Storm clouds were hurrying across the sky, letting more and more blue show through. In New York, the climate—or should I say the weather—changes fast and often: having the ocean nearby makes the patterns unpredictable.

That's enough about blood.

[Addendum: Bob Kelly, theatrical supplier, is a real person, and his business is well known in New York. But he's not on Second Avenue, as the author has described. His address is 151 West 46th Street, and you take the elevator to the ninth floor, not the sixth.]

EPILOGUE

One addendum opens the way for more. Although this novel is over and done with, many issues remain unresolved.

I've already covered the symbolic significance of the journey to Helsinki.

A lot of text was dedicated to Poder, who then disappears from the story entirely. I saw him getting on a bus once, but that's it. I know nothing more of him or his plans.

I've met that talkative schoolteacher again, here and there, but his concerns touch on subjects that are beyond the scope of this epilogue.

That stage director was pure invention.

On a road at night we met a young boy, just for a moment. Grown by now, he went to school, and became familiar with modern teaching methods. The end.

Joosep?

There are signs that show he's still around. A couple of years ago a general strike was organized on the Tallinn Railway. They say the hole in the ozone in the northern hemisphere is only getting larger. Last autumn the stores were out of lightbulbs. In a forest near Iru, the corpse of an unknown man was discovered. My blood pressure is a little higher than the average. But these are only signs. Sadly, I have nothing concrete to report.

This spring I saw another swarm of dawn butterflies.

Minni is still dear to me.

At her suggestion I've added a few other items of interest:

Adults tolerate blood loss much better than children.

Women tolerate loss of blood better than men.

Lean people tolerate loss of blood better than the obese.

Elevating a wounded limb decreases the flow of blood to the afflicted area.

When two incompatible blood types are mixed, the transfused blood goes into erythroblastosis, resulting in serious trauma, and sometimes death.

Preferred blood donors are healthy persons between twenty and forty years old.

Blood regeneration is facilitated by high calorific food.

Love comes in by way of the stomach.

Who loves, lives long.

During a long enough life one is liable to witness any number of incredible events.

But sometimes nothing happens.

The surface of water is still.

When the wind doesn't blow, sand doesn't fly.

And light is always bluer or redder than it should be.

October, 1989

SELECTED DALKEY ARCHIVE PAPERBACKS

PETROS ABATZOGLOU, *What Does Mrs. Freeman Want?*
PIERRE ALBERT-BIROT, *Grabinoulor.*
YUZ ALESHKOVSKY, *Kangaroo.*
FELIPE ALFAU, *Chromos.*
    Locos.
IVAN ÂNGELO, *The Celebration.*
    The Tower of Glass.
DAVID ANTIN, *Talking.*
ANTÓNIO LOBO ANTUNES, *Knowledge of Hell.*
ALAIN ARIAS-MISSON, *Theatre of Incest.*
DJUNA BARNES, *Ladies Almanack.*
    Ryder.
JOHN BARTH, *LETTERS.*
    Sabbatical.
DONALD BARTHELME, *The King.*
    Paradise.
SVETISLAV BASARA, *Chinese Letter.*
MARK BINELLI, *Sacco and Vanzetti Must Die!*
ANDREI BITOV, *Pushkin House.*
LOUIS PAUL BOON, *Chapel Road.*
    Summer in Termuren.
ROGER BOYLAN, *Killoyle.*
IGNÁCIO DE LOYOLA BRANDÃO, *Teeth under the Sun.*
    Zero.
BONNIE BREMSER, *Troia: Mexican Memoirs.*
CHRISTINE BROOKE-ROSE, *Amalgamemnon.*
BRIGID BROPHY, *In Transit.*
MEREDITH BROSNAN, *Mr. Dynamite.*
GERALD L. BRUNS,
    Modern Poetry and the Idea of Language.
EVGENY BUNIMOVICH AND J. KATES, EDS.,
    Contemporary Russian Poetry: An Anthology.
GABRIELLE BURTON, *Heartbreak Hotel.*
MICHEL BUTOR, *Degrees.*
    Mobile.
    Portrait of the Artist as a Young Ape.
G. CABRERA INFANTE, *Infante's Inferno.*
    Three Trapped Tigers.
JULIETA CAMPOS, *The Fear of Losing Eurydice.*
ANNE CARSON, *Eros the Bittersweet.*
CAMILO JOSÉ CELA, *Christ versus Arizona.*
    The Family of Pascual Duarte.
    The Hive.
LOUIS-FERDINAND CÉLINE, *Castle to Castle.*
    Conversations with Professor Y.
    London Bridge.
    North.
    Rigadoon.
HUGO CHARTERIS, *The Tide Is Right.*
JEROME CHARYN, *The Tar Baby.*
MARC CHOLODENKO, *Mordechai Schamz.*
EMILY HOLMES COLEMAN, *The Shutter of Snow.*
ROBERT COOVER, *A Night at the Movies.*
STANLEY CRAWFORD, *Some Instructions to My Wife.*
ROBERT CREELEY, *Collected Prose.*
RENÉ CREVEL, *Putting My Foot in It.*
RALPH CUSACK, *Cadenza.*
SUSAN DAITCH, *L.C.*
    Storytown.
NICHOLAS DELBANCO, *The Count of Concord.*
NIGEL DENNIS, *Cards of Identity.*
PETER DIMOCK,
    A Short Rhetoric for Leaving the Family.
ARIEL DORFMAN, *Konfidenz.*
COLEMAN DOWELL, *The Houses of Children.*
    Island People.
    Too Much Flesh and Jabez.
RIKKI DUCORNET, *The Complete Butcher's Tales.*
    The Fountains of Neptune.
    The Jade Cabinet.
    Phosphor in Dreamland.
    The Stain.
    The Word "Desire."
WILLIAM EASTLAKE, *The Bamboo Bed.*
    Castle Keep.
    Lyric of the Circle Heart.
JEAN ECHENOZ, *Chopin's Move.*
STANLEY ELKIN, *A Bad Man.*
    Boswell: A Modern Comedy.
    Criers and Kibitzers, Kibitzers and Criers.
    The Dick Gibson Show.
    The Franchiser.
    George Mills.
    The Living End.
    The MacGuffin.
    The Magic Kingdom.
    Mrs. Ted Bliss.
    The Rabbi of Lud.
    Van Gogh's Room at Arles.

ANNIE ERNAUX, *Cleaned Out.*
LAUREN FAIRBANKS, *Muzzle Thyself.*
    Sister Carrie.
LESLIE A. FIEDLER,
    Love and Death in the American Novel.
GUSTAVE FLAUBERT, *Bouvard and Pécuchet.*
FORD MADOX FORD, *The March of Literature.*
JON FOSSE, *Melancholy.*
MAX FRISCH, *I'm Not Stiller.*
    Man in the Holocene.
CARLOS FUENTES, *Christopher Unborn.*
    Distant Relations.
    Terra Nostra.
    Where the Air Is Clear.
JANICE GALLOWAY, *Foreign Parts.*
    The Trick Is to Keep Breathing.
WILLIAM H. GASS, *A Temple of Texts.*
    The Tunnel.
    Willie Masters' Lonesome Wife.
ETIENNE GILSON, *The Arts of the Beautiful.*
    Forms and Substances in the Arts.
C. S. GISCOMBE, *Giscome Road.*
    Here.
DOUGLAS GLOVER, *Bad News of the Heart.*
    The Enamoured Knight.
WITOLD GOMBROWICZ, *A Kind of Testament.*
KAREN ELIZABETH GORDON, *The Red Shoes.*
GEORGI GOSPODINOV, *Natural Novel.*
JUAN GOYTISOLO, *Count Julian.*
    Makbara.
    Marks of Identity.
PATRICK GRAINVILLE, *The Cave of Heaven.*
HENRY GREEN, *Blindness.*
    Concluding.
    Doting.
    Nothing.
JIŘÍ GRUŠA, *The Questionnaire.*
GABRIEL GUDDING, *Rhode Island Notebook.*
JOHN HAWKES, *Whistlejacket.*
AIDAN HIGGINS, *A Bestiary.*
    Bornholm Night-Ferry.
    Flotsam and Jetsam.
    Langrishe, Go Down.
    Scenes from a Receding Past.
    Windy Arbours.
ALDOUS HUXLEY, *Antic Hay.*
    Crome Yellow.
    Point Counter Point.
    Those Barren Leaves.
    Time Must Have a Stop.
MIKHAIL IOSSEL AND JEFF PARKER, EDS., *Amerika:*
    Contemporary Russians View the United States.
GERT JONKE, *Geometric Regional Novel.*
JACQUES JOUET, *Mountain R.*
HUGH KENNER, *The Counterfeiters.*
    Flaubert, Joyce and Beckett:
    The Stoic Comedians.
    Joyce's Voices.
DANILO KIŠ, *Garden, Ashes.*
    A Tomb for Boris Davidovich.
ANITA KONKKA, *A Fool's Paradise.*
GEORGE KONRÁD, *The City Builder.*
TADEUSZ KONWICKI, *A Minor Apocalypse.*
    The Polish Complex.
MENIS KOUMANDAREAS, *Koula.*
ELAINE KRAF, *The Princess of 72nd Street.*
JIM KRUSOE, *Iceland.*
EWA KURYLUK, *Century 21.*
VIOLETTE LEDUC, *La Bâtarde.*
DEBORAH LEVY, *Billy and Girl.*
    Pillow Talk in Europe and Other Places.
JOSÉ LEZAMA LIMA, *Paradiso.*
ROSA LIKSOM, *Dark Paradise.*
OSMAN LINS, *Avalovara.*
    The Queen of the Prisons of Greece.
ALF MAC LOCHLAINN, *The Corpus in the Library.*
    Out of Focus.
RON LOEWINSOHN, *Magnetic Field(s).*
D. KEITH MANO, *Take Five.*
BEN MARCUS, *The Age of Wire and String.*
WALLACE MARKFIELD, *Teitlebaum's Window.*
    To an Early Grave.
DAVID MARKSON, *Reader's Block.*
    Springer's Progress.
    Wittgenstein's Mistress.
CAROLE MASO, *AVA.*
LADISLAV MATEJKA AND KRYSTYNA POMORSKA, EDS.,
    Readings in Russian Poetics: Formalist and
    Structuralist Views.

FOR A FULL LIST OF PUBLICATIONS, VISIT:
www.dalkeyarchive.com

SELECTED DALKEY ARCHIVE PAPERBACKS

FOR A FULL LIST OF PUBLICATIONS, VISIT:
www.dalkeyarchive.com